Dark
SUSPICIONS

ANNE SCHRAFF

URBAN UNDERGROUND®

SADDLEBACK
EDUCATIONAL PUBLISHING
www.sdlback.com

© **2012 by Saddleback Educational Publishing**

ISBN-13: 978-1-61651-958-2
ISBN-10: 1-61651-958-4
eBook: 978-1-61247-646-9

Printed in Guangzhou, China
NOR/1213/CA21302313

18 17 16 15 14 2 3 4 5 6

CHAPTER ONE

Naomi Martinez lay on the grass in the small garden in their backyard on Bluebird Street. Her father, Felix Martinez, had designed it. Mr. Martinez was a tough, often harsh man. He operated heavy equipment for a construction company. He had three sons—Orlando, Manny, and Zack. At one time, he had driven them all off. But now the boys were speaking to him again, thanks to Naomi and her boyfriend, Ernesto Sandoval.

Ernesto sat on a stone bench in the garden. He was looking at an endearing little elf that Felix Martinez had carved. The pretty little garden, filled with elves and flowers, was nothing like Mr. Martinez's personality.

"That was so horrible last night," Naomi remarked, turning to look at Ernesto. "That kid getting shot. I woke up and heard sirens, and I just got sick."

"Yeah," Ernesto responded. "Coach Muñoz is counting on Julio Avila and me to lead the track team to victory. I've got to get in some running. I got rusty over the summer. I get in my best running at night. Now Mom is giving me a hard time about that."

"What about during the day?" Naomi asked.

"I'm at school, and I got so much work with the AP History. Then I go to work. I told Mom not to worry. The guy who was shot caught a random bullet. Some idiot was doing target practice or something, and the kid got in the way," Ernesto said. "It's not like there's a crazy sniper loose in the *barrio*."

"We hope," Naomi sighed, glancing up at the clouds. They were so beautiful today. One minute they were like gossamer and the next minute like swollen bags of thunder and lightning. Like people. Always changing. Unpredictable. "Lucky the boy just got a bullet in the leg. It could have been so much worse. What if he'd been hit in the head?" Naomi shuddered.

"Yeah," Ernesto agreed. "It had to be some fool, maybe reloading a gun or something. I figure the dude got rid of the gun when he realized what happened. He'll probably never shoot again. But he's too scared to come forward and own up to what he did. He's probably shaking in his boots. He's afraid the cops are gonna knock on his door any day now."

"The boy who got shot," Naomi commented, "his name is Alex Acosta. I don't know him, but Carmen Ibarra said her father knows the family. She said they're nice people. Alex goes to the community college. He's not a gangbanger or anything. No drugs. When he was shot, the family just went into shock."

"I'm just hoping it blows over," Ernesto said. "I need to go running again. If I don't

3

get up some speed before the next meet, I won't be much good to Coach Muñoz. And what really sticks in my craw is Rod Garcia being on the team. He didn't do much running until this year. That was right after I beat him in the senior class president election. I think he joined the team just so he could stick it to me. Ever since I was elected senior class president over him, he tries to make me look bad any chance he gets."

"That is so childish," Naomi replied.

"Yeah, he never misses a senior class meeting," Ernesto added. "He's always raising his hand and offering some lame advice or criticizing what we're doing. He was so sure he was gonna win the election. Then this upstart—me—comes down from Los Angeles and takes it away from him." Ernesto shook his head.

"Ernie," Naomi said, "you're doing such a great job for the seniors. That *compañeros* program where the kids help each other out, it's wonderful. School spirit is really up this year. It's like everybody isn't just in it for themselves. We all feel like we're making it to the finish line together."

"I wish Rod could see it that way," Ernesto sighed. "People are strange."

At Cesar Chavez High School the next day, Ernesto ran into another member of the Cougars track team, Jorge Aguilar. He was a good runner, but he never had the speed of either Ernesto or Julio Avila.

"Hey, Jorge," Ernesto called, "you get in much practice? The next track meet will be coming up before we know it. I lost a lot of speed over the summer. I'm trying to do stretching exercises and run a lot to get my mojo back."

Jorge shrugged. "I got work and school. I'm thinking about dropping track It's just not worth it to me," he replied.

"Sorry to hear that, man," Ernesto said. He looked more closely at his friend. Jorge was a nice kid. But last summer he was hanging out with some older guys, and they were all smoking weed. Ernesto

5

heard about it from Paul Morales. Paul was manager of an electronics store, but he had a lot of connections to wannabe gangbangers. He knew what was going on in the *barrio*.

"Jorge said he didn't like the stuff, and it was a one-time thing," Paul had told Ernesto. "But that's what most of them say."

"You doing okay, Jorge?" Ernesto asked. "You look kind of wasted."

"I'm fine," Jorge replied.

"Look, if you need help with any of your classes," Ernesto told him, "you know where to go. We're all in the home stretch now, man. We're heading for that graduation day. We don't want to lose anybody now."

"Yeah, thanks," Jorge said. He spotted his close friend, Eddie Gonzales, and he walked toward him.

"Jorge, don't quit the track team until you've really thought about it, dude," Ernesto called to him. "It's great exercise, homie, and we all like you. It won't be the same with the Cougars if you're not with us."

Jorge turned briefly and gave Ernesto a thin smile. "Thanks, man," he responded.

That night, Ernesto worked his shift at the pizza shop. When it was over, he jumped into his old Volvo and drove home. Both his parents were in the living room watching the ten o'clock local news.

"Something going on?" Ernesto asked, glancing at the screen. It didn't look like anything exciting.

"No," Maria Sandoval, Ernesto's mother answered. "We both needed to take a break before we went to bed."

Ernesto didn't believe his mother. Since that dude got shot, they worried when Ernesto wasn't home at night. "You know, you guys," Ernesto commented, "when I drove home tonight, the streets were totally empty. No gangbangers hanging around. The police did those gang sweeps last month, and it's gotten a lot better. I think it's pretty safe now to do a little running. I need to be ready for the meet."

Mom frowned. "Gangbangers are like cockroaches," she declared. "You don't know how many of them are hiding in dark corners until you shine a light. Then there's a million of them crawling around. Just because you don't see them doesn't mean they're not there."

"Yeah," Luis Sandoval, Ernesto's father, agreed. Mr. Sandoval was a teacher at Cesar Chavez High. "The police haven't gotten the guy who shot Alex Acosta yet." Ernesto's father also taught part-time at the community college. Alex was in his American history class.

"I don't know when Alex will be able to come back to school," Mr. Sandoval went on. "He's a good student. Luckily the bullet went through the leg without major damage. He'll heal quickly. But the psychological damage, that's a whole other thing. Once you get shot like that, you're not the same. I can't help but think the gangs had something to do with it."

"Honey," Mom said, "we'd just feel better if you didn't jog at night. I mean at least not until they find out who shot that boy on Washington Street."

"Okay, Mom," Ernesto responded. "Maybe some jerk'll come forward and admit he was shooting at a stray cat or something. Maybe the kid just got in the way."

"Discharging a firearm is a serious crime," Ernesto's father remarked. "I'm not so sure any run-of-the-mill guy would be doing something like that."

Luis Sandoval was a much-loved history teacher at Chavez. He not only ran exciting classes but showed a real interest in his students. And he also went out of his way to search out dropouts and try to bring them back to school. He often walked to the park in the evenings and joined kids in basketball games. He became one of the players and gained the confidence of the boys.

Then he talked to them about resuming their education. He had lured quite a few back to Chavez. But he didn't do that anymore after the shooting. Luis Sandoval had a wife, two sons, and two little girls to think about. He wasn't looking for trouble.

Alex Acosta had been shot on a Friday night, two weeks ago. According to Alex, he had just stopped at the twenty-four-seven store to buy a soda. He was walking down Washington Street when suddenly he heard a loud noise. At the same moment he felt a bad sting in his calf. He looked down at his jeans and saw a lot of blood oozing from one pant leg.

Alex said he looked around and didn't see anybody. He slumped down to the curb and called 911 on his cell. The paramedics arrived to find him trying to stop the bleeding. He had made a makeshift tourniquet out of his belt. He was bleeding heavily, and the tourniquet didn't do much good. Alex told the police that he didn't see who shot him. The bullet seemed to come out of nowhere. The police recovered the bullet near where Alex was shot. It had gone clear through his calf.

Alex was taken to the emergency room of the hospital, and he spent two days there before being released. There was no serious damage, but he had to stay off the leg for a while. Alex Acosta told the police he had never belonged to a gang, and he didn't even know any gangbangers. He said he was shocked and scared about what happened. He didn't think he had any enemies.

Ernesto thought it was strange that Acosta wasn't back to school on, say, crutches.

And he wasn't surprised that someone had been shot in the *barrio*. He and his family had moved back to the *barrio* last year from Los Angeles. In LA, they had lived in a better neighborhood, but the school where his father taught was downsized. Mr. Sandoval lost his position and found a new job at Cesar Chavez High.

To Ernesto's parents, the *barrio* was home. They had both grown up here and had moved to Los Angeles when Ernesto was small. They were home, where they had lived as children and young adults. Dad's family still lived around here.

But to Ernesto last year, it was a scary place. Graffiti was all over on the fences and the sides of buildings. Gangs roamed the streets. The first few weeks Ernesto lived here, he was scared. Once, as he was coming home from the pizzeria where he worked, two guys jumped him. They wanted to know what gang Ernesto belonged to.

Ernesto could still feel the sheer terror as one of the guys grabbed him around the neck from behind. The guy in front wore a hoodie, and he had a lot of tattoos. He wanted to know whether Ernesto was Eighteenth Street. Ernesto gasped that he didn't belong to any gang.

Ernesto silently prayed as his *abuela* did—*Madre de Dios, ayudame*!

The gangbanger released Ernesto and shoved him, pushing him to his knees.

The two guys vanished into the darkness. Ernesto recalled his feeling of pure relief. He didn't even mind that his jeans were bloodied at the knee where he'd hit the sidewalk.

Since then, Ernesto had had no problem. There were robberies and gang fights in the *barrio*. The police helicopters hovered overhead. Guys with warrants on them got busted. But generally Ernesto felt pretty safe.

On the weekend, Ernesto put the shooting of Alex Acosta out of his mind. He went to the automobile show with Abel Ruiz, Paul Morales and Cruz Lopez. They drove down in Cruz's wildly decorated van. The van was splashed with peace signs, colorful animals and flowers, and some other stuff Ernesto didn't understand.

"I hope the cops don't stop us," Cruz remarked. "They're thicker than ants on a watermelon slice since that kid got hit."

Paul laughed. "You ain't got any warrants on you, do you, homie?"

"A parking ticket maybe," Cruz admitted. "It mighta blown off my windshield the other day."

Paul laughed harder. "They ain't gonna bust us over that, homie."

Paul turned to Ernesto. "You fixing to replace that Volvo with one of these dream machines at the auto show?" he asked.

"I wish, dude," Ernesto moaned. "Maybe one of these days I'll turn the Volvo in on a late-model sports car or something like that."

"I got my eye on a sweet sedan, dudes," Paul declared. "I've seen it, and it's got some cool extras. Even the outside mirrors are heated so they don't fog up. And it's got a seven-speaker XM-CD-MP3 audio system. Man, me and Carmen could really cruise in that baby."

Abel shook his head. "It's like thirty thousand or something," he groaned. "I'm gonna be driving my Jetta until the wheels fall off. After I graduate Chavez, I got culinary school, and that's not cheap. I think I got a good shot at a scholarship, but I gotta save some money anyway."

"Yeah," Ernesto agreed. "No dope sedans in my future either. I gotta go to college, then law school. Man, the road ahead stretches out. Dad's a great teacher, but he doesn't make big bucks. No teacher does. Mom makes a little on her children's books, but my college is gonna mostly be what I save and loans. Maybe a scholarship for some of it."

"I'm not rolling in it either," Paul said. "But I'm saving money from my salary. I'm manager now at the electronics joint, and I got a coupla little projects on the Internet. I might be able to handle that sedan if everything comes out right for me."

Ernesto and Abel both gave Paul a long look. Cruz glanced quickly at him, even though he was driving.

"You're not steppin' over the line, are you, man?" Abel asked.

Paul laughed again. "I got a brother in prison, homie. He messed with the Man, and I sure learned from that. I'm not goin' down that road."

They parked in the underground lot at the convention center. As they got out of the van, Ernesto asked, "How's it going with you and Bianca, Abel?"

Abel smiled a little. "We're having a good time. She's the kind of a girl you can feel comfortable with. We're just good friends, and that's the way we both like it. I got in over my head once. I'm not going there again anytime soon."

"I stopped in the Sting Ray the other day," Paul said. "My boss at the electronics store took me there for sushi. There was a real hot chick sashaying around."

"That'd be Cassie," Abel remarked.

"Yeah?" Paul grinned. "She giving Bianca any competition for your heart, *amigo*?"

"No," Abel protested. "She's hot all right, but she leaves me cold. She reminds me of my mom. Any guy gets her, he's gonna be whittled down to size real quick. But she did tell me I sorta looked like James Dean." Abel waited for the other boys to start laughing.

Cruz didn't know who James Dean was, but both Paul and Ernesto knew. They had seen *Rebel Without a Cause*.

"Dude," Ernesto commented, "your eyes . . . they do sorta look like his eyes."

"Yeah," Paul agreed. "The Latino James Dean. Ay! But seriously, man, you don't look half bad. Last year you had a lot of zits. Now that that's all cleared up, you sorta got that James Dean angst look. But don't go flying down the highway like he did, homie. He left this planet way too soon."

"No chance o' that," Abel said. "I'm a dorky driver. When guys pass me on the road, they glare in the driver's side. I guess they expect to see a little old lady or an old dude wearing a hat. They can't believe it's a young guy."

Ernesto laughed. "Yeah, have you guys noticed? When an older guy is wearing a hat, he drives like a snail. It can be any kinda hat—a baseball cap, a straw hat."

Paul Morales led the boys to his dream sedan right away. "Hey, homies," he exclaimed as they neared the car, "is that a beauty or what? And it's red!"

A beautiful girl in a very short red skirt walked over to them, her gaze focusing on Paul. "I see you like our car," she noted. "That color is called a red jewel tint coat. It's only about three hundred dollars extra. Everybody says it's candy apple red, and it looks good enough to eat."

"Sure thing," Paul responded. "You look good enough to kiss, babe."

The girl giggled, appreciating the compliment from a very handsome young man. Ernesto had to admit it. Of the four guys, Paul was the hottest dude. Also, Paul looked a little older than the others and more likely to be able to afford the car.

After the girl moved on to another group, Ernesto turned to Paul. "Paul, do you do stuff like that when you're with Carmen?"

"Stuff like what?' Paul asked. "Complimenting a hot chick? Carmen understands. She's a hot chick too. She knows she doesn't have to worry about a thing."

They weren't allowed to drive the car. But they could sit in it and feel what that was like. Paul got behind the wheel next to Cruz and Ernesto, and Abel sat in the back.

"The center console is a little bit in the way. It got my knee," Cruz remarked. "I don't think I'll buy one today. The van has got to do."

"Plenty room back here," Abel commented. "Man, cup holders and seatback pockets to store your burritos."

"You stick burritos in my car's pockets," Paul warned in fun, "and I'll pulverize you, homie. I *want* this car."

Ernesto and Abel exchanged a look. Where was Paul getting enough money to even dream of getting this car?

CHAPTER TWO

After they had seen all the cars, the boys walked back to the parking lot.

As they climbed into the van, Ernesto looked over at Paul. He asked warily, "When do you think you can buy the car, dude?"

Paul Morales answered, "Well, either I can boost one sometime soon. Or else I may have to wait a few years. I guess having one Morales boy in the slammer is enough. So I think I'm gonna choose the second option."

Ernesto smiled at Abel with relief. Ernesto never really believed Paul was into something illegal. But with Paul he could never be completely sure about anything. "When's your brother getting out, Paul?" Ernesto asked.

"He's been doing real good," Paul replied. "He might get out in a few months. He's really with the program. He's dotting all the i's and crossing all the right t's."

Paul's face lit up with a smile. "You know those films I've been making? Well, my teacher, Anisa Lee—that's the chick who took me and some other of her students to Sundance last year. Well, she suggested I make a documentary about David. You know, how he went down the wrong road. Then how he's taken all those college classes in prison, and now he's a computer geek. It'd be raw and real. It might even get some of the homies with rap sheets to believe they can turn things around too. I talked to David about it, and he's cool to do it."

"Sounds good, man," Ernesto agreed.

"Yeah," Paul nodded. "David's the only relative I've got in the world, dude. He's my brother. We didn't do much growing up together 'cause we were mostly in different foster homes. But we got a bond. We're

21

tighter than a lot of brothers who grew up in the same house."

"I hear ya, homie," Abel responded, thinking of his own brother, Tomás. They grew up together, but Abel was always jealous of Tomás. Mom kept holding him up as the perfect son that Abel could never be. Mom kept harping on Tomás's achievements and Abel's failures. Mom drove a wedge between the boys, and Abel doubted that he and Tomás could ever be close. Now, all Abel wanted to do was put as much geography as possible between him and his brother.

The van was coming down Washington Street, near Tremayne. Cruz would turn there to drop Ernesto and Abel off at their houses.

Ernesto pointed out the window. "Hey, is that Jorge Aguilar over there by the twenty-four-seven store?"

The boy's back was turned, but it sure looked like Jorge.

Jorge was talking to two older guys, and they were all smoking. The windows of Cruz's van were open, and the four boys recognized the familiar smell. They all knew what Jorge and his friends were smoking.

"Grass!" Paul said with disgust.

"Jorge's talking about dropping off the track team," Ernesto remarked. "I think he's probably sweating the drug tests the athletes at Chavez take. Look, Cruz, we're almost at my street. Just let me off here. I'll walk the rest of the way home. I want to have a word with Jorge. He's a good guy, and I hate seeing him sucked into the sewer."

"You sure, dude?" Cruz asked. "I don't like the looks of those two creeps with the kid. I'm pretty sure they're gang members. You sure you want to mess with them?"

"It's okay," Ernesto insisted. "Just drop me at the corner. I want to talk to Jorge. I won't say anything to the gangbangers."

"Not a good idea, homie," Abel advised grimly.

"No, no," Ernesto protested. "I know what I'm doing."

Cruz pulled to the curb, and Ernesto slid the door open, getting out. "See you guys later. Thanks for the ride to the auto show, Cruz."

Cruz continued down Tremayne Street, where he was dropping Abel off at his house on Sparrow. Then Cruz and Paul planned to hang out together for a while.

Ernesto approached the trio in front of the twenty-four-seven store. "Hey, Jorge," he called in a pleasant voice. He didn't recognize the two guys with Jorge. They looked quite a bit older than Jorge, probably in their twenties. One had a ratty-looking goatee, and the other was gaunt, wasted on something stronger than grass. "Maybe heroin," Ernesto thought. Heroin was making a comeback in the *barrio*.

Jorge and the other two headed down the alley with Ernesto in pursuit. "Hey, Jorge, I just want to talk to you, man," Ernesto called, catching up to the three.

"Get lost, man!" Jorge snarled in an angry voice. It wasn't his normal voice. That's not the way Jorge talked to Ernesto or to *anybody*. Ernesto figured he was trying to impress his new friends.

"Who's he?" the one with the goatee snarled. He looked at Ernesto with narrowed, bloodshot eyes.

"Just some dude from Chavez," Jorge answered. "His old man's the history teacher there."

"Jorge," Ernesto said, "you got too much going for you, man. You shouldn't be standing around the street smoking dope with a coupla losers."

"Dude," the wasted-looking guy said in a menacing voice, "is this the mountain you want to die on?"

"I think this fool needs a lesson," the goateed man said, coming at Ernesto.

Ernesto grabbed his cell phone to call 911. But then the two men tackled him. The phone went flying as they slammed Ernesto to the ground on his back.

25

"Gonna kick your face in, dude," the goateed one hissed. "You won't be so pretty no more when we get done."

In the next second, three figures came out of nowhere. One of them hurled Jorge against the wall of a building. The other two came at the man with the goatee and his friend. Ernesto saw a switchblade in the gaunt one's hand, but in an instant it was wrenched away. Switchblades flashed in the hands of the three newcomers, and the gangbangers took off running. Jorge lay on the asphalt, winded.

Ernesto got to his feet. His three friends were next to him. Ernesto noted they each had switchblade. He'd never seen a blade in Abel's hand.

"Told you it wasn't a good idea to stop and talk to Jorge," Abel said as he closed the blade and returned it to Cruz.

"You guys," Ernesto gasped, shaken by how close he'd come to having his face broken. "How'd you know to come back?"

"Ernie," Paul chided in a scornful voice, "you got more heart and courage than you got common sense. We turned around right away and headed back. We all knew what was going down. Maybe if Jorge'd been all alone smoking dope, you mighta had a chance. Maybe your goody-two-shoes sermonizing coulda done him some good. But those other two dudes weren't about to listen to preaching. They've sold their souls to *el Diablo*."

Paul stooped and picked up Ernesto's phone. "Won't be texting or talking on this baby anytime soon."

"You know those guys, Paul?" Cruz asked.

"I didn't from a distance but up close, yeah," Paul responded. "The guy with the goatee is called Cabron, and the pale one is Simon. They've got rap sheets going way back, but they know how to game the system. They plea-bargain and work with slimy lawyers, and they're bounced back on the street. They won't get put away till they put some poor devil in the ground."

Cruz turned to Jorge. "You sure know how to pick 'em, fool!"

Jorge looked scared. "I wasn't with them," he stammered. "I don't even know the dudes. I was passing by and they offered me a little pot, y' know. I wasn't with them."

Paul grabbed Jorge's shirtfront and rammed him back against the wall. "You weren't with them, punk? You coulda fooled me. You looked like you were a gangbanger just like them. Cabron just missed being busted for intendin' to commit murder two months ago! You hear me? Anybody in his camp woulda got busted along with him."

Paul gave Jorge a hard shake. "You got no brains, punk? You lay down with dogs, you get up with fleas. You listening to me?"

Then Paul turned to Ernesto. "Where does this fool live?"

"On Finch," Ernesto answered. "I drove him home one day after track. I know the house."

"Okay," Paul declared, "let's load this piece of garbage in the van and dump him off with his folks. Maybe his old man is good with his fists."

"You can't tell my father what happened," Jorge cried. "He'll kill me!"

"Works for me," Paul replied. "Save the taxpayers some money when a coupla years from now you're up for some felony." Paul's voice was calm, but he had an evil glint in his eye.

The van stopped in the driveway of the Aguilar home. It was a well kept up stucco house, like most in the neighborhood. There were a lot of red geraniums in the yard.

"You want to explain to the Aguilars what went down, Ernie?" Paul asked. "We don't want to all barge in."

"Sure," Ernesto agreed, getting out of the van and going to the door. He'd already met the Aguilars. It was at a Saturday picnic that Coach Muñoz threw for his track team and their parents. Ernesto remembered a tired-looking mother and an overweight dad.

Mr. Aguilar came to the door. He remembered Ernesto as one of the track team members of his son's team. "Eddie?" he asked. "Eddie Gonzales?"

"Ernie Sandoval," Ernesto replied.

"Oh yeah, yeah, the history teacher's kids," the man recalled. "Hey, you're the big honcho down there—the senior class president." The man smiled a little. "What's up?"

Then he glanced at the van and saw his son. His smile vanished. "What's up?" he asked again, this time nervously. "Something wrong?"

"Mr. Aguilar," Ernie responded, "we're all worried about Jorge. He's been talking about quitting the track team. Just now we caught him smoking dope with two really hardcore bad guys . . . older guys. Gangbangers."

The man blanched, then his face turned red. He pushed open the front door and sprinted to the van. He slid the door open with a bang and grabbed his son's shoulders, hauling him out. "You lousy little creep!" he screamed. "Where you get off hanging with gangbangers? Your ma found the dope in your room last week, and you swore you'd never do it again. You wanna get busted? You wanna break your mother's heart?"

"Pa, I didn't even know the guys!" Jorge blurted. "I was on my way home, and these dudes just started talking. I wasn't smoking no dope—"

"He was smoking dope," Paul told the father. "He was hangin' with the gang-bangers like they were blood brothers. I know the slippery slope, man. I got a brother doing time 'cause he went down the same road. Only this little creep has no excuse 'cause he's got a nice home. Me and my brother grew up in foster homes where nobody wanted us."

Mr. Aguilar looked hard at the boys who had brought his son home. "Thanks, you guys," he said sincerely. "Thanks from the bottom of my heart. You had my boy's back, and I'm grateful. This here bum is our only son. I got two daughters, but this here is my only boy. If I lost this kid to the streets, I might as well pack it all in, you get my meaning?" The man's voice was heavy with emotion.

"Good luck, man," Paul said to man.

Mr. Aguilar dragged Jorge up the driveway, pushed him in the front door, and slammed the door behind them.

As the four boys were getting into the van, they heard Jorge scream.

Ernesto felt a little sick. He hated violence. He'd never seen it in his own family. He hated the thought of what was now going on in the Aguilar house. Ernesto couldn't even dream of his own father beating him for any reason.

Paul looked at Ernesto and saw the anguish on his face. Paul grabbed Ernesto's upper arm and gave it a squeeze. "Hey, homie, it's okay," Paul assured him. "Don't get the guilts. We did the right thing. Don't look so sad. The kid has a beating coming to him."

Paul saw he wasn't getting through to Ernesto. He looked out the van windows and started talking. "I don't remember

much of what I learned in school. But a
middle school teacher —a mean lady—she
told us this story. It was about this kid in
the Midwest. He had an awful temper.
When things didn't go his way, he freaked.
One night his old man wouldn't let him go
trick-or-treating like he wanted. He flew
into a rage. Well, his old man cut a switch
from a tree and whipped the kid good."

Paul glanced over to Ernesto, who was
staring out the other window. Paul felt that
his friend was listening. Paul went on.

"Now, I know beatin' on kids is wrong.
But in those days, parents did it, not as
abuse but as discipline. That's just the way
they saw things. Anyway, the whippin'
made a man outta the boy. He grew up to be
a famous general. Guy helped win World
War II. And then he got to be President
Dwight David Eisenhower. He made it all
the way to that big White House in Washington. Y'hear me, Ernie?"

Ernesto didn't say anything, but he
shrugged his shoulders.

Cruz dropped Ernesto off at his house, and he walked in slowly. It had been a good day at the auto show until they saw Jorge Aguilar with the gangbangers.

Nobody was home in the Sandoval house. Mom had taken little Alfredo and his sisters to the doctor for a checkup. *Abuela* was visiting friends at church. Ernesto didn't know where his father was.

Ernesto sank into a soft cushioned chair. He closed his eyes. He could still hear that guy with the goatee swearing to kick his face in as he lay on the ground. What if Abel, Paul, and Cruz hadn't shown up? Ernesto thought he'd probably be in the emergency room right now getting his jaw wired—or worse. They might have kicked in his skull.

Ernesto was numb with gratitude to his friends. He felt it before, and now he felt it again. Nobody on earth had better friends than he did. Ernesto swore to himself that he'd never fail them if any one of them needed his help.

34

When Mom came home, she asked Ernesto, "How was the auto show, honey?"

"Good, Mom. We saw some great cars," Ernesto replied.

A moment's silence followed. Ernesto always marveled at how his mother could detect something was wrong. How hard he tried to conceal it did no good. She gave Ernesto a long look. "What happened?" she asked him.

"I uh . . . dropped my cell phone, and now it's busted," Ernesto answered, trying to keep his voice light. "I guess you could say it's road kill."

"You look like you've been in a fight, Ernie," Mom noted. "There's dirt all over your shirt."

Ernesto had been knocked to the ground by the gangbanger. He never thought to change his shirt before Mom came home with her eagle eye.

Ernesto pressed his fingers against his closed eyes. He sighed. Then he said,

"Mom, you know the Aguilars . . . Jorge's on the track team with me."

"Yes, I know," Mom said. "What happened with Jorge?"

"He's been weird lately," Ernesto explained, "talking about dropping track. Mom, he's always enjoyed it so much. But he's started smoking dope. Me and the guys were coming home from the car show, and we saw Jorge with a couple of gangbangers on Washington. Real bad dudes. Jorge's okay. He's not a punk."

Ernesto looked up at his mother and continued. "Well, when I ran for senior class president at Chavez, I promised to do my best to get all the seniors through. You know, so we'd all be there together on graduation day. So, like I get out of Cruz's van and go over to talk to Jorge. I want to get him away from those gangbangers."

Ernesto drew a long breath. "Anyway Jorge didn't want to hear what I had to say. And the other two, the gangbangers, they sorta jumped me."

"Oh my God!" Maria Sandoval cried.

"It's okay, Mom," Ernesto assured her. "The guys—Abel, Paul, Cruz—they came on like the U.S. Cavalry in those old Westerns. They helped me out, scared the gangbangers off. Then we got Jorge home. So it ended up okay."

Mom's eyes were wider than usual. "How did your friends drive off dangerous gangbangers, Ernie?"

"Uh, I guess they had switchblades," Ernesto murmured.

"*Ayyy!*" Mom gasped. "Who? Paul? Cruz? Surely not Abel?"

"Well, Cruz tossed him one too," Ernesto admitted.

"Ernie! Ernie!" Mom groaned. "You go to a nice auto show at the convention center, and you end up in a gang fight!"

"It's okay, Mom," Ernesto cried.

"No, it's *not* okay," Mom insisted. "If you thought Jorge was in trouble, you should have called the police. This is over your head, Ernie. You can't be

37

doing things like this. It's bad enough that your father goes out in the dark to play basketball with wannabe gangbangers, the riffraff of the *barrio*! That terrifies me enough. Now you appoint yourself the guardian of all the seniors at Chavez High School."

Mom plopped down on the sofa and briefly buried her face in her hands. "There I was, making sure the girls and Alfredo had their shots on schedule. I was happy as a clam. And my son has a deadly confrontation with criminals!"

"I'm sorry, Mom," Ernesto sighed. "I did something stupid. Abel and Cruz told me not to do it, and I won't do anything like that again."

Mom finally looked up. "You took Jorge home?" she asked.

"Yes. His father was there. I told him what happened," Ernesto replied.

"What did he say?" Mom asked.

"He thanked us for getting Jorge away from those guys," Ernesto answered. "And

38

then, you know, as we were driving away, we heard Jorge yelling. I think his dad was laying into him."

Mom got a strange look on her face. "I know Mrs. Aguilar," she commented. "I don't know her husband too well. She's a good woman, and she told me her husband is a good man. So I'm not going to judge what he does. I just hope Jorge has learned his lesson."

"Yeah, me too," Ernesto agreed. Jorge's scream was still haunting him.

"Honey," Mom said, "I know you mean well, but you can't save the whole world. You're just like your father, but there are limits. Thank God you're all right. All I know is, I've got a splitting headache."

CHAPTER THREE

Later that afternoon, Ernesto's grandmother, *Abuela* Lena, was sitting in her room. She was by the window, watching the sparrows hopping around the backyard. She smiled at Ernesto when he came into the room. She had broken her hip a little while ago, but she was recovering nicely. She was using a walker only as a precaution. Soon she'd need only a cane.

"You know, Ernie," *Abuela* remarked, "when I was your age, my *abuela* would tell me she spent a lot of time thinking about the past. She thought a lot about the good times she'd had. I thought this was so strange. Why would anybody want to think of the past? Wouldn't it make them sad to think of days gone by? But now I understand. I love to remember when your father and all our children were little. How much fun we had. The *fiestas* in the *barrio*. How the children screamed with joy breaking the *piñatas*. The past is like drawing close to a warm fire on a winter's day. It warms me and delights me to remember."

Ernesto sat down in a chair opposite his grandmother. "I'm glad you came to live with us, *Abuela*, he told her. "It means so much to Katalina and Juanita too. They'd rather be with you than almost anyone else, because you got time for them. Mom is trying to squeeze in her next book about the lizards and taking care of the baby."

Just then Maria Sandoval came into the room with her baby son, Alfredo, in her arms. "Mama," she asked, "would you take him for a little while? I have one more chapter I need to finish on the computer. I need to send it tonight."

"Of course," Lena Sandoval agreed, taking Alfredo and cradling him in her

41

arms. He seemed happy. "I love babies," the woman remarked.

Alfredo went to sleep in his grand-mother's arms, as Ernesto continued to sit quietly.

"I was scared when we first moved here, *Abuela*," Ernesto confided in a hushed voice. "But now I love the *barrio*. I love Cesar Chavez High too."

"Yes, you are senior class president!" Lena Sandoval replied in an excited whisper. " I am so proud of you, Ernie."

"I like the job," Ernesto commented. "It makes me nervous sometimes when I have to lead those meetings. Some of the kids resent me. Not many, but a few. They make a lot of noise. But the thing is, my friends are so great. I remember when I first drove on campus in my old Volvo. A lot of kids were laughing at me, but then Abel and his buddies stood with me. One of the guys backing me up was Jorge Aguilar. I'm not real close with Jorge. But we're on the track team together, and he's a friend."

Ernesto took a deep breath and went on. "The guy's gotten mixed up with some bad dudes. I got involved and almost got my head knocked off, but my friends helped me. I gotta admit I've had second thoughts about that. I coulda got killed trying to rescue Jorge from those gangbangers."

Lena Sandoval continued gently rocking the sleeping baby in her arms, but her lined face grew serious. "Ernie, I remember years ago when your *abuelo* and I lived in this *barrio*. Your father and my other children were going into their teens. Your father had a friend, Ricky. Ricky was not a bad boy, but he was always getting into trouble. He made bad choices. There was a drug problem. In those days we called the drug addicts 'heads.' Their guns were called 'pieces,' and there was graffiti just like now."

Abuela turned her gaze to the sparrows again. She was seeing the past. "Well, the only good boy Ricky knew was Luis Sandoval, your father. My husband didn't want our son getting mixed up with this troubled kid. So he wouldn't let Ricky come to our house anymore. After that, Ricky just went downhill. I often wonder what would have happened. What if we had allowed your father to continue being his friend, fighting to get him on the right path. Maybe Luis could have saved Ricky if your *abuelo* had let the friendship continue. Maybe not. But I often wonder."

Ernesto stared intently at his grandmother. "Did you ever find out what happened to Ricky?" he asked.

"He got deeper into the gang," Lena Sandoval replied, in a soft voice. "They called themselves the Delaware *Diablos*. One night they got involved in a fight with another gang. It was Halloween night. This little boy was trick-or-treating with his brothers, and they got caught in the crossfire. The child was killed."

The old woman's head nodded slowly. "Ricky and another boy went to prison for murder. He's still there—a life term.

Maybe Ricky would not have been on the street that night if Luis had his way. Maybe he would have been shooting baskets in our driveway with Luis." Her voice trailed off.

"Thanks, *Abuela*, for telling me about this," Ernesto said softly. "I think maybe I needed to hear it."

Ernesto dreaded school on Monday. If Jorge Aguilar was there, Ernesto wasn't sure how he'd react. How would he feel about being dragged home for a beating? Maybe Jorge hated Ernesto for what he'd done. Maybe he'd never talk to Ernesto again—or do something worse.

Or maybe Jorge was so angry that he'd left home. Maybe he was hanging in the ravine with some other lost souls. Maybe right now he was smoking dope in the ravine called Turkey Neck off Washington. That ravine was the end of the road for many losers on the run from angry and desperate parents, and for old dopers and mentally ill men.

Jorge's closest friend at school was Eddie Gonzales. They hung out together more than with anybody else. When Ernesto saw Eddie coming on campus, he walked over nervously.

"Hey, Eddie, wassup?" Ernesto asked, hoping for some information on Jorge. Jorge texted Eddie all the time over minor things. But maybe he was so ashamed of what happened that he didn't text anybody about it.

"Nothin', man," Eddie replied, glancing around. "I'm looking for Jorge. He's usually here by now. He's been talking about dropping the track team, and I gotta talk him out of it. It wouldn't be no fun for me if we weren't both there. I texted him all weekend, but he never got back to me. That's not like Jorge."

Ernesto was now more worried than ever. Jorge had never complained to anybody about his father being a brutal man. That was something guys weren't anxious to share. Getting a whipping from your father when you were a senior in high school had to be humiliating. Ernesto kept remembering hearing Jorge yelling in pain after the door of the Aguilar house slammed shut.

"Oh, there's the dude now," Eddie pointed. "He's at the vending machine. He loves those chocolate chip cookies."

Ernesto didn't know whether to face Jorge now or duck over to his first class and postpone seeing him. Ernesto wasn't the kind of guy who pushed off anything, even when he feared the results. Putting things off just gave him more time to brood. So Ernesto and Eddie walked over together to the vending machine. Ernesto thought that, as long as he was with Eddie, Jorge wouldn't poke him one.

Jorge turned when Eddie called to him. "Wanna run after school today, man?"

"Yeah, maybe," Jorge mumbled. Just then Eddie spotted his girlfriend coming on campus, and he ran to meet her, leaving Ernesto and Jorge alone.

"Look dude," Ernesto said, "I'm sorry if—"

"Don't sweat it, homie," Jorge cut him off, sampling one of the chocolate chip cookies in the small bag he bought. "I was talking tough in front of those gangbangers, but I was shaking in my sneakers, man. I'd bought some junk off of them once, and they were pressuring me to sell it at Chavez. I was in way over my head by the time you showed up. They were leaning on me pretty hard."

"I was worried about how you made out at home," Ernesto said.

"My old man knocked me around a little bit, but it was okay," Jorge shrugged. "You know the saying, dude. What doesn't kill you makes you stronger." He smiled ruefully. "As you can see, I ain't dead. I know my father cares a lot about me. The dude was crying while he was hitting me. Man, that was worse than the blows, I'm telling you."

Jorge was speaking in a dead serious tone. "Believe me, I'm staying away from those creeps now. I'm gonna stay clean.

When Coach Muñoz springs that drug test on me, I'm gonna ace it. Cabron, he texted me already. I told him my old man almost killed me. I ain't messing with it no more."

"Those guys pushing pot in the *barrio*?" Ernesto asked.

"Pot, heroin, rock coke, oxycontin, anything," Jorge replied. He smiled then. "Man, Ernie, you got some tough homies. When they flashed their blades, Cabron and Simon took off like brush rabbits. Especially that dude, Morales. I think he could scare *el Diablo* into going back to hell."

That night Ernesto talked to his father about what Jorge told him.

"I'll tell Arturo," Dad responded. "My brother knows a lot of police on the narcotics squad. A lawyer gets to meet those guys. I don't want those drug peddlers to get a foothold in the *barrio*. Time for some sweeps."

"Dad," Ernesto remarked, "your mom told me about when you were a kid. About some dude named Ricky."

Luis Sandoval took a deep breath. "I think you and I need to take a walk, *mi hijo*."

Whenever father and son had something important to talk about, they took a walk together. They both grabbed sweaters because it was a little chilly outside.

The stars were brilliant in the clear sky, and the crescent moon was horizontal. It looked like a big smile in the sky. Wren Street was dark and quiet.

Dad began by saying, "Ricky was always full of mischief. I met him in first grade. We were close after that. He always did stuff most of us wanted to do but were too chicken to do. He brought his pet tarantula to school in Ms. Peebles room and let it out."

Luis Sandoval smirked and shook his head. "The poor woman almost had a stroke. Ricky got in fights too. Usually lost because he was small . . ."

50

"Did he start the fights?" Ernesto asked.

"Yeah," Dad responded. "He had a speech defect, and kids would make fun of him. Then he'd be off and running. He was good enough in school, but he was what they'd now call 'speech impaired.' He always gave twice as much as he got. Some kid would mock him, and he'd hit that kid so hard his nose would spurt blood."

Dad was thoughtful for a second and then spoke. "It got worse in middle school. Ricky got busted several times. Mama felt sorry for him. But my father really worried that Ricky's bad ways would rub off on me and bring me down."

They had reached Tremayne and turned onto it.

"Were you his best friend, Dad?" Ernesto asked.

"His *only* friend, I guess," the father replied. "We both wanted to play professional basketball. We loved the Lakers. I think our best day was when we got to go to a Lakers championship game. But neither of us were good enough for the NBA. Dad decided I shouldn't hang out with Ricky anymore. He wasn't welcome at our house."

"Grandma told me about that," Ernesto commented. His father nodded to acknowledge what the boy had said. Then he went on.

"It was sort of a turning point in Ricky's life. He joined the Delaware *Diablos*. The gang was named after Delaware Street. Anyway, October—Halloween—we were both fifteen, almost sixteen. A gang fight led to the death of a little boy. His candy was spilled all over the street . . . little kid, maybe eight."

"*Abuela* said Ricky took the fall for it," Ernesto said.

"Him and another boy, yeah," Dad nodded yes. "The crime outraged the neighborhood. Boys were tried as adults. I tried writing to Ricky. Even then I didn't want him feeling totally abandoned. He never answered me. I've tried a couple times since with no luck." Dad sighed deeply.

"That's why I was trying to keep Jorge out of the soup, Dad. Did Mom tell you what happened on Saturday?" Ernesto asked carefully. His mother usually shared important stuff with Dad.

"Yes, she told me." the father answered. "I'm glad she did. I don't keep secrets from her, and she doesn't keep them from me. That's death in a relationship, Ernie. Remember that. You know, though, what your mom told me kinda shook me up. I didn't know your friends carried switchblades. That's serious business. Something could go wrong, and a guy could get killed." Dad turned and looked grimly at Ernesto.

"It was good at the time, though, Dad. The police can't be everywhere. One of the gangbangers had a blade, and all my homies had to do was open theirs up. Those dudes were ready to kick my brains out."

"Yeah, Ernie, but learn from that," Dad advised. "Don't put yourself in dangerous situations like that. I know, I do stuff I shouldn't be doing too. But if you see something bad going down, call nine-one-one."

"I tried to do that, Dad," Ernesto responded. "But this gangbanger decked me in a split second and smashed my phone. But you're right, I was stupid getting into it. Paul and Abel and Cruz warned me, but I dove in anyway. I think sometimes I'm too full of myself."

"As long as you learned from it," Luis Sandoval told his son, throwing his arm around the boy's shoulders. "Like I said, I'll go over to the school and get in a basketball game, even though I see gangbangers on the street. I charge into a bunch of kids thinking I can convert them to truth and goodness. And a coupla times they almost took me on."

As they turned and started for home, Ernesto asked, "Is that dude who got shot back in his classes at the community college yet, Dad?"

"No," Mr. Sandoval answered. "I texted him and offered to e-mail him class work.

That way, he can keep up until he can come back. But I got no answer. I don't know what's up with the guy. Is he just spooked so bad by what happened that he's given up on school?"

"Seems crazy to let all his plans for the future go down the drain. And all just because he was in the wrong place at the wrong time. He just walked into a stray shot," Ernesto noted.

"Unless that's not what happened," Dad suggested.

Ernesto turned and stared at his father. "You think somebody shot him on purpose?" he gasped.

"I don't know, Ernie. But the past few days that Alex attended classes, he seemed strange," Dad mused. "He's a good student. But we had a test, just a routine quiz that even the poor students aced. Alex blew it completely. He wasn't himself. Something was on his mind. I know he told the police that he had no idea who might've shot him. He had no enemies and all that. But I'm not completely believing it. Alex seemed scared and preoccupied that last day."

Ernesto and his father walked in silence, each with his own thoughts. Eventually, they neared their turn off Tremayne. As they did, two police cars careened by, their lights and sirens going. Ernesto felt a sudden pang of fear. "They're turning down Bluebird, Naomi's street, Dad!" he gasped.

"There are over twenty houses on Bluebird," Ernesto's father advised. "Take it easy."

At a quicker pace, they soon reached Bluebird. There, they saw the police cars parked by the house across the street from the Martinezes. Felix Martinez and Naomi were standing in their front yard watching.

"What's going on, Felix?" Luis Sandoval called, approaching the yard.

"Something bad happened at the Torres place," Mr. Martinez reported.

Just then a fire engine and an ambulance came down the street, also stopping at the Torres house. Ernesto knew Roxanne

Torres. She was a senior at Chavez High. One time, Felix Martinez and his son, Zack, were battling it out in the front yard of their house. Roxanne took pictures on her cell phone and was about to put them online when Ernesto stopped her.

Other neighbors on the street had come out to watch the excitement.

"Somebody shot in there," a man announced.

"Who?" Luis Sandoval asked. "Do you know who's shot?"

"They're saying the girl who lives there got shot," the man replied.

Naomi turned to Ernesto, shock on her face. "Roxie? I wonder if Roxie got shot, but who—"

The paramedics went in, wheeling a gurney from the rear of the paramedic truck. After a long while, they came out with someone on the gurney and put the person in the vehicle. They didn't seem to be calling for a helicopter, so Ernesto hoped the injuries weren't serious.

Suddenly a dark sedan came speeding up to the house. A man and woman rushed from the car into the house.

"That's Mr. and Mrs. Torres," Felix Martinez remarked. "Roxie's parents. I guess they weren't home when whatever it was happened. Maybe the kid was alone . . ."

Mrs. Torres was crying hysterically when she came out of the house and climbed into the ambulance with her daughter.

All kinds of wild thoughts flashed through Ernesto's mind. Maybe Roxanne was monkeying with a gun, and it went off by accident. Maybe an intruder found the girl home alone and shot her.

The police were swarming around the house for a long time. Apparently, they were checking for footprints or signs of forced entry. Ernesto thought it must have been a prowler. Eventually a police sergeant addressed the large crowd now gathered. "Folks," he announced, motioning with his arms, "there's nothing to see here. Go back in your houses, and clear the streets. There could be an armed and dangerous person around."

"Let's go," Luis Sandoval commanded. "Maybe the shooter's still in the neighborhood."

Naomi came over and squeezed Ernesto's hand. "I'll call you the minute I find out anything, babe," she told him.

When Ernesto and his father got home, Maria Sandoval was listening to the television news. "They've got breaking news," she reported in a tense voice. "A shooting over on Bluebird Street, right down the block. And you two are wandering around out there! I'm telling you, between the two of you, you're making me old before my time!"

"We're fine, Mom," Ernesto assured her. "Something happened at the Torres house, across from Naomi's place. It sounds like Roxanne was home alone and somebody got in and shot her. Her folks just got home a little while ago. They took Roxie off in an ambulance."

Mom's eyes widened until they looked twice their normal size. "Roxie Torres was shot? Right in her own house? My Lord, what is this world coming to? That is so terrible, so frightening!" Mom was quaking.

The Sandovals didn't know the Torres family well. They'd met infrequently at parent-teacher meetings Cesar Chavez High School. The Torres had one daughter—Roxanne—a fair student who liked to gossip more than anything else. She always had her iPhone ready to snap somebody doing something embarrassing. She shared the pictures with her friends and sometimes online. Maybe, Ernesto thought, somebody out there didn't want their picture to see the light of day.

CHAPTER FOUR

The next morning, the Sandovals watched the early news on television before Ernesto and his sisters went to school. The glum–looking anchorwoman spoke to them from the screen.

Eighteen-year-old Cesar Chavez High School senior, Roxanne Torres, is recovering in the hospital today after a terrifying experience at her home last night. According to the girl, she was home alone last night and napping on the living room couch around nine. An intruder entered the house, and, when she saw him, she screamed. The intruder shot Roxanne in her upper arm. She is expected to make a full recovery.

She's listed in satisfactory condition at Memorial Hospital, where she was able to give police a detailed description. The intruder is still at large. He is about forty years old. He has a shaved head and a long thin face with a prominent scar on his chin. The initial police sketch is now on your screen.

"What a horrible experience for that poor girl," Maria Sandoval cried. "To wake up to see that awful man with a gun in her house!"

"He probably figured no one was home," Ernesto said, shaking his head. "He figured he'd just grab what was easy to find and get out of there. And then Roxie sees him and screams."

"I wonder if they keep their doors locked," Dad said. "A lot of people are careless about that. They just leave the door unlocked all day until they go to bed at night. If it looks like nobody's home, it's a big temptation for thieves."

Katalina had stopped eating her breakfast burrito. She was staring at the television screen as the newscast once more showed the police sketch. "That guy looks awful, like a monster in a creepy movie," she commented.

"He won't come here, will he?" Juanita asked.

"We always keep our doors locked," Mom assured her. "So we don't have to worry about someone just coming in."

Ernesto thought the sketch of the intruder looked vaguely like someone he knew. He just couldn't place him. He'd seen someone recently who strongly resembled the guy in the sketch. Maybe it was one of the vagrants who came up from the ravine and begged for money in front of the stores.

"Fortunately the girl is going to be okay," Mom announced. "I called her mom last night and asked if there was anything I could do. I'm not close to Mrs. Torres, but they're practically neighbors. She told me Roxanne will have to wear a sling for a while, but she should be fine."

During his time at Chavez High, Ernesto had had little to do with Roxanne Torres. He remembered she was in his junior English class last year. She was always talking to her seatmates and drawing the ire of Ms. Hunt. Roxanne made poor grades, as Ernesto recalled, but she always squeaked through. She was one of the oldest seniors at Chavez, almost nineteen now. Roxanne liked boys, and she seemed to know what was going on in everybody else's life. When Ernesto thought of her, he could hear her high-pitched voice. She was always saying, "You guys, you won't believe what I just heard!"

"It's really frightening, though," Mom added, "that a criminal would be bold enough to go into a house when he isn't sure there's nobody home. I don't remember that ever happening around here."

Ernesto loaded his sisters into the Volvo, and they headed for their schools. His sisters seemed very upset by the crime over on

Bluebird Street. It was all they could talk about. Ernesto tried to change the subject.

Ernesto dropped the girls at their school, then drove the short distance to Chavez High.

When Ernesto came on campus, he saw a large group of students in animated conversation about the shooting. In the middle of the group was Clay Aguirre, and—as usual—he seemed to be doing most of the talking. Ernesto went to the edge of the crowd and listened.

"You guys, it's a no-brainer," he was saying. "When I saw that police sketch on the TV, I yelled out to my dad, 'That's him!' I know that dude. Same long thin face, bald, the scar on his chin from some knife fight. That's the lousy bum who hangs out behind the twenty-four-seven store. Those dumb immigrants let him crash there. It's Griff Slocum. I always knew the creep was dangerous."

Ernesto stiffened. The sketch had looked familiar to him too, but he couldn't place the person. But, sadly, Clay was right. The sketch looked just like Griff Slocum. There was no arguing with that. But Griff was a poor harmless man who was even too shy to ask for money. All the other panhandlers in the *barrio* were way more aggressive. Sometimes Ernesto and Abel would buy him a sub sandwich and a cup of coffee. And Griff, his eyes downcast in shame, would thank them. Ernesto always figured he'd been an ordinary working stiff a long time ago. Perhaps some terrible circumstances had brought him down, and he couldn't find his way back up. To imagine Griff Slocum invading the Torres house and then shooting Roxanne seemed unbelievable.

"Griff Slocum could have never done that crime," Ernesto protested. "The guy is afraid of his own shadow. He doesn't have a violent bone in his body."

"Oh, listen to Mr. Know-it-all," Clay sneered. "Even before you got to be senior class president you had an ego as big as the Pacific Ocean. Now you got that job, and you think you're the wisest dude in the

66

world. But you're not. You're a bleeding heart jerk, Sandoval, who lives in a fairy-land where there are no bad guys. Well, most of the homeless bums are psychos. They're liable to go off at any minute and get violent. They're like wild animals."

Mira Nuñez, who used to date Clay Aguirre before she got tired of his verbal abuse, piped up. "It sure does *look* like that Slocum guy. I've given the guy some change, and he seemed harmless enough. But I guess you can't tell with those people."

"I've tipped the cops already," Clay announced. "They need to haul that creep in before he shoots somebody else. Like he shot a chick! They got him for attempted murder!"

Abel joined Ernesto at the edge of the crowd. "It looked like Griff," he told Ernesto. "The sketch did, but I'm with you, Ernie. He didn't do it. One time I put some leftovers from one of our dinners at the Sting Ray—some fried shrimp we never served—in a plastic container and gave it to Griff. He was so grateful, he almost cried."

Rod Garcia, who disliked Ernesto for beating him for senior class president, threw in with Clay. "I hope the cops nab Slocum quick. I've always thought all those homeless dudes should be arrested."

Ernesto and Abel gave up and walked toward their morning classes.

"I feel sorry for Griff," Ernesto remarked. "He's probably had a lousy life so far. Now the cops are gonna go down there and arrest him and haul him off to jail for something he didn't do. The poor guy is gonna be scared out of his wits."

"Yeah," Abel agreed. "But what I can't figure is, how come that sketch looks so much like the dude?"

Ernesto had a hard time concentrating in his history class. Rod Garcia was answering all the questions Mr. Bustos posed. When Ernesto did speak up, he made a mistake. He got James Madison mixed up with Alexander Hamilton.

By the time Ernesto got home from track practice, the television news stations were reporting the latest development. A person of interest had been taken into custody in the shooting of Roxanne Torres.

Ernesto made a sandwich of leftovers and walked down to the twenty-four-seven store. He wanted to see what he could learn about what happened. He went in the store and smiled at Hussam, who was behind the counter. He sometimes gave Griff small odd jobs so that he could earn a little spending money.

"Hey, Hussam, something happen to Griff?" Ernesto asked.

"Yeah. How'd you know?" Hussam asked. "The cops came and took him away."

"Somebody at school told the cops about him," Ernesto explained. "The sketch of the guy who shot the girl on Bluebird Street, it looked like Griff. I know Griff didn't do that crime, though."

"I don't believe it either," Hussam agreed. "He was crying and shaking when the cops took him away. But, you know, lotta pressure on the cops to solve this thing. When some kid gets shot in her own house . . . I never hear of it happening around here. In Baghdad, yeah. When we hear shots, we dive for cover. There, yes, but not on Bluebird Street."

Ernesto went on to Naomi's house. He was surprised to see Roxanne in the front yard of her house, talking to Naomi. Her arm was in a sling, but she looked fine otherwise. She was rattling on as she always did. Ernesto remembered Ms. Hunt calling her "motor mouth."

"Hey, Roxie," Ernesto hailed, joining the two girls. "How're you doing?"

"I guess as good as can be expected after such a horrifying experience," Roxanne replied. "Man, I don't think I'll ever completely get over what happened. It was the scariest experience of my entire life. I was watching this boring movie on TV, and I fell asleep. All of a sudden, I woke up, and this monster was staring at me with a gun!"

Ernesto always thought his good friend, Carmen Ibarra, talked too much, but Roxanne had her beat.

"I see this horrible man, ugly, with a skinny face and a scar in his chin," she rattled on. "He looked like a skeleton. I'm telling you, it was like a horror movie. You ever see that movie *Scream*? Oh man, he looked like that creature. I screamed, and then he shot me. I guess he panicked or something 'cause he ran. Ohhh! The pain. It was unreal. I thought he'd shot my arm off. The blood . . . ohhh! I screamed and screamed, and then I finally got the strength to call nine-one-one. I told them some guy tried to kill me. Ohhh! I almost died of fear."

Naomi glanced at Ernesto. "Roxie thinks that homeless man who hangs around on Washington was the intruder . . . Griff Slocum," Naomi told him.

"You've seen Griff at the twenty-four-seven store. Right, Roxie?" Ernesto asked.

"Yeah," the girl responded. "He always gives me the creeps. When I see him, I cross the street so I don't have to get close to him. He makes my skin crawl, the way he demands money and threatens people when they don't give it to him. It was dark in the room when I was shot, but I'm pretty sure it was Slocum. It looked exactly like him."

"Roxie," Ernesto said softly, "Griff never asks for money. He's real shy. He's skittish around people. Even if you give him something, he like looks down like he's ashamed to be taking anything."

"All those horrible creatures who live on the street ask for money," Roxanne insisted. "I don't know why the police let them stay there harassing people. They should all be rounded up like feral cats and locked away."

"Roxie, Griff Slocum is disabled," Naomi said. "His speech is garbled, and he limps. I don't know what happened to him years ago, but he's kind of pathetic."

"I think all those guys are just too lazy to work," Roxie ranted. "They pretend they're disabled and stuff, but they just want to get money from other people. They're parasites. That's what my father said."

Ernesto glanced at Naomi who rolled her eyes. "Roxie, something awful happened to Griff years ago," he told her. "I don't know what it was, but he's not a normal person anymore. But that doesn't mean he's evil or dangerous. I don't know who came in your house and shot you, but I don't think it was Griff Slocum. I don't think the guy would even know how to use a gun."

Roxanne tossed her head angrily. "Oh, Ernie!" she protested. "Everybody says you're so tolerant of creepy people. Well, he didn't come to *your* house and shoot someone in your family. He didn't shoot one of your sisters or Naomi. He came to *my* house and shot me. I guess I have the right to hate him and want him put away for good."

"The police will get to the bottom of it," Naomi declared. "Anyway, Roxie, I'm glad you're feeling better."

"I'm not feeling all that much better, Naomi," Roxanne insisted. "I've been traumatized. I doubt I'll ever be the same after this. I'll be like those soldiers who're in battle in Afghanistan. You know, they get half blown up. So when they come home, they got this battle stress or something. That's what I've got. I'm just all messed up. I may need to see a doctor and go into therapy and stuff."

"Well, I hope you feel better soon, Roxie," Naomi said. She grabbed Ernesto's arm and propelled him across the street to her house. She was really eager to get away from Roxanne.

"Mom bought some biscotti, Ernie," she told him. "And it's really good with cappuccino. You've got to have some. Dad's crazy about it."

Ernesto and Naomi went into the Martinez house, and Mom brought out the biscotti and cappuccino. Felix Martinez was sitting in his favorite easy chair, enjoying some of the biscotti.

"Hey, Ernie, how's it goin'?" he asked cheerfully. He seemed in a very easygoing mood, considering what had happened to Roxanne across the street. Ernesto expected Felix Martinez to be in a rage that the police had allowed such a terrible crime to happen on his street. Ernesto thought Mr. Martinez would be worrying about a similar attack on his house with Naomi being in danger.

"I'm doing okay, Mr. Martinez," Ernesto replied. "But how are you holding up with all the excitement across the street the other night."

Linda Martinez, Naomi's mother, brought more biscotti and cappuccino. She also seemed unconcerned about the violence at the Torres home.

Felix Martinez leaned forward and looked at Ernesto. "Just between you and me and the gatepost, Ernie." His head swiveled left and right a couple of times. "I ain't buying that little twit's story, if you know what I mean." He had a snide grin.

Linda Martinez chimed in. "Roxanne is a terrible liar. Some of the stories she's spread are disgraceful."

"So what do you think happened?" Ernesto asked eagerly.

Mr. Martinez leaned back in his chair and got more comfortable. "Well, she's got too many boyfriends," Naomi's father stated scornfully. "Too many little punks comin' and goin' when the idiot parents are off doing their thing. The parents, they ain't too swift. They think they got a sweet little princess over there. They think she's all the time doin' her homework and stuff like that. But soon as I see the parents goin' off, it ain't long before the little punks start arriving."

Ernesto looked at Naomi. Naomi never mentioned Roxanne's social life, but Naomi wasn't the gossip that Roxanne was. Now Naomi admitted, "Roxanne likes boys a lot."

"Don't she ever," Felix Martinez crowed. "And she ain't too particular either.

Some of them look like something the cat dragged in. I'm thinkin' some greasy little weasel come by the other night. They got some horseplay goin', and the punk was showin' off and the gun went off. I think it was an accident. So Roxie—being Roxie— is not going to admit to anythin'. She's not gonna say she had a punk over, and he shot her by mistake. Ya know why? Because Mommy and Daddy can't handle the truth, y'know? So little Roxie does what she always does when she's in a tight spot. She lies. She cooks up this big story about the big bad monster comin' in and shootin' her. And, don't you know, she ends up smellin' like a rose."

Mr. Martinez bobbed his head, as if to say, "You know I'm right." Then he chomped another bite of biscotti.

"But," Ernesto protested, "the police have already collared some poor dude because he looks like the composite sketch Roxanne gave the police. I mean, this is awful. If it didn't even happen, then an innocent man is being harassed. You think she'd do this to cover her own backside?"

"In a New York minute, Ernie," Mr. Martinez asserted. "You're a good kid, Ernie. You're solid gold. My own boys, they got their warts, but deep down they got character. But this Roxie, you don't know how rotten people can be. This creepy little chick across the street has the major hots for one of those jerks who comes visit her. But she wants to stay out of trouble with her dopey parents. She wants to save her punk boyfriend from getting into trouble for firing off a weapon that hit somebody. Hey, you think she'd hesitate to throw some poor hopeless dude under the bus? Not on your life, Ernie."

Ernesto was furious. Of course, he didn't know whether any of Felix Martinez's suspicions were actually true. Maybe none of it happened the way he was telling it. After all, he didn't have any proof.

Ernesto thought maybe Naomi's father was blowing smoke. Mr. Martinez didn't like the Torres family anyway, especially Roxanne. He knew she'd taken pictures of him and Zack fighting that night and was going to put them online. It was easy for Mr. Martinez to think the worst of the girl. And yet, for Ernesto, the story had the haunting ring of truth to it.

After Ernesto had some more biscotti and cappuccino, he went outside with Naomi to say goodnight.

"Naomi, what do you think of what your dad is saying?" he asked her.

"Dad can be off the wall a lot of times, but, Ernie, I almost believe him," Naomi answered. "But what can we do? Poor Griff Slocum has nobody to defend him, and he looks so bad."

"When I get home, Naomi, I'm calling my Uncle Arturo," Ernesto declared. "I'm telling him everything. If anybody can help Griff, he can."

Later, Ernesto got his uncle on the phone and explained the situation. Arturo Sandoval responded, "Ernie, I'll talk to the police on the case, and I'll see Mr. Slocum. We'll see where it goes."

"Thanks, Uncle Arturo," Ernesto said, flooded with warmth and admiration for his father's brother.

Ernesto Sandoval's desire to become a lawyer was fueled by his respect for his uncle. If anyone in the *barrio* was in trouble and an injustice might be underway, Uncle Arturo was instantly involved. Ernesto was deeply relieved that Griff Slocum now had somebody on his side.

CHAPTER FIVE

After the call to his uncle, Ernesto thought about what Mr. Martinez had said. Ernesto never remembered seeing Roxanne Torres at school with a steady boyfriend. She flirted with boys at the track meets and at lunch, but she never seemed to pair up with any one boy.

Ernesto called Carmen Ibarra on his cell phone. Carmen usually had the scoop on who was hanging with one another.

"Carmen," Ernesto said as soon as she answered the phone, "I been thinking about Roxie Torres. You know, her getting shot and all? The cops nabbed that homeless dude, Griff Slocum, because he looks like the intruder Roxie described. But I think he's innocent."

"Yeah," Carmen agreed. "Dad's never gotten a complaint about him. He's so peaceful." Carmen's father, Emilio Zapata Ibarra, was a city councilman. People were always complaining to him and other members of the council about aggressive panhandlers.

"Carmen, somebody was taking to me about maybe Roxanne's story being bogus," Ernesto continued. "She's saying some older guy shot her. Okay, but maybe she was accidentally shot by one of her own boyfriends, and she's covering up for him. I was wondering, Carmen, I've never seen Roxie tight with anybody at Chavez. Does she have a steady boyfriend that you know of?"

"She goes with older boys, Ernie," Carmen replied. "Even when she was in middle school, she hung out with guys from Chavez. Now that she's almost nineteen, she dates guys who're done with school, or maybe quit school a long time ago. She has kind of a creepy taste in guys."

"Well," Ernesto admitted, "I don't know, of course, if she was shot by a boyfriend and now she's lying. That's just a theory of somebody I know. But one thing I'm pretty sure of, Griff Slocum never busted in there and shot the girl. That just doesn't hold water."

"Yeah," Carmen agreed. "Hussam is always giving Griff little jobs to keep him going, and he's so grateful. Hussam told me once Griff is like a child, like a hurt little kid. Know what, Ernie? I'll ask Paul if he knows anything about the dudes Roxie's hanging with. I'll have him call you if he has any idea."

"Thanks, Carmen," Ernesto said. It was true that Paul Morales knew the underbelly of the *barrio*. Roxie might have had some wannabe gangbanger for a boyfriend who might have been showing off his gun that night. If so, Paul might know the dude's name.

Before Paul Morales got back to Ernesto, Uncle Arturo called. He didn't sound upbeat.

"Ernie," the man said, "the police found pot on Griff—a lot of it. They're going to charge him with possession. They don't have anything linking him to the shooting, but they're keeping him on ice while they investigate. Ballistics has already turned up something disturbing. My friend on the case said the bullet taken from Roxanne Torres' arm was from the same gun used to shoot that college student, Alex Acosta. The crimes are linked. I'm worried, Ernie. Sometimes drugs twist a man's mind. Griff could have been using other even more potent drugs. He's a gentle man by nature, but you never know when dangerous chemicals are introduced."

Ernesto felt sad as he thanked his uncle and closed the phone. Ernesto disliked Clay Aguirre, but what Clay said at school about Ernesto had a grain of truth. Ernesto always *did* give people the benefit of the doubt. Ernesto didn't live in a fairyland, as Clay said, but he did believe in the basic goodness of most people. Deep in his heart he'd always believed that Griff Slocum was a good man. Griff was a victim of circumstances largely beyond his control. But maybe that wasn't true. Maybe Griff had a dark side that Ernesto had not seen. Maybe he fired the random shot that hurt Alex Acosta. Maybe he somehow stumbled into the Torres house and shot Roxanne.

Paul Morales pulled up to the Sandoval house in his pickup truck in the early evening. Ernesto's parents liked Paul, but they weren't too thrilled with their son's close friendship with him. He was too rough, too much on the edge. He had strange friends, and he carried a switchblade. He had a brother coming out of prison soon after being several years inside the walls. Paul wasn't the kind of a young man Ernesto's other friends were, guys like Abel and Julio. Paul had a rattlesnake tattooed on his hand, and his flashing dark eyes had a disturbing violent streak.

That was why Carmen Ibarra's parents were unhappy when their beloved daughter fell in love with Paul. That was why it was awkward for Ernesto, too, when Paul came into the Sandoval living room, where Mom and Dad scrutinized him with wary looks. *Abuela* did not seem to feel that way. She always had as warm a smile for Paul as for everybody else. Katalina and Juanita looked at Paul Morales with unseemly admiration, as a dashing creature from the wild side. They couldn't get enough of how he made the rattlesnake on the back of his hand jump by making a fist. They squealed with delight.

When Ernesto saw Paul outside in the driveway, he said, "Oh, there's Paul. Me and him are going to look at some cars. I'm going to be replacing the Volvo one of these days."

"Oh!" Mom said. "Well, be careful."

Ernesto hurried outside and jumped into Paul's truck. Inside the cab, Ernesto threw a question at Paul.

"Did Carmen—?"

"Yeah, she told me everything," Paul replied.

"I found out," Ernesto said, "that the same gun that shot Roxanne Torres was used to shoot that college guy, Acosta. What do you make of it, Paul?"

"I've seen the Torres chick over at the Cat's Paw. That's a not-so–kosher watering hole over on Polk," Paul answered.

"I know the place," Ernesto noted. "Adults only."

"Yeah, part strip joint, part booze bar," Paul explained. "I was with Carmen one day, and we saw this kid going in with an older dude. So I'm going to Carmen, 'Hey, what's with that? They let kids in that dive now?' And Carmen said, 'That's Roxie Torres. She's almost nineteen. She lives across the street from Naomi, and she's a senior in high school.' Well, lotsa dirtbags hang out in there. The chick mighta picked up a boyfriend there."

Paul was getting worked up. "I seen some really bad guys around there. Simon,

Cabron, those creeps who were tryin' to make mush outta your head, Ernie. Remember when you rescued Jorge from them? I've seen Cabron doing drugs right on the street in front of the Cat's Paw. He and the other dudes scatter like rats when the cops finally show up."

"I'm really surprised Roxie's parents let her run with that crowd," Ernesto commented.

"Lotta parents don't get it, man," Paul countered. "They're clueless. I see a lotta chicks eighteen, nineteen hangin' out at the Cat's Paw. Maybe they're runaways or maybe they're throwaways, you know? Or maybe, like this Roxie chick, she just does her own thing, and her parents are zoned out on tranquilizers. So they don't worry."

Paul mused for a while and then spoke again. "Reminds me of that sick little chick, Elena's daughter. When we worked at the doughnut shop, the lady let her run wild, and in the end she's dead of an overdose in a ravine."

88

"Paul," Ernesto asked, "that college guy, Acosta. You think he's into drugs? He said—"

"I've seen him buying, dude," Paul stated flatly.

"Oh man! He came off as a nice, innocent guy, clean as a whistle, the victim of a random shooter," Ernesto said with a shudder.

"I never believed that," Paul insisted. "I think he got into a fight over dope he was buyin' or sellin'. Carmen told me that her father, good old Councilman Ibarra, knows the Acosta family. They're the salt of the earth. But, homie, the world is changed. Cops come to the door to tell parents that their kid is busted, and they're clueless. The parents don't want to believe what's going down. They want to think the world was still like those good old days. You know, when high school kids got busted for chewing gum in class and sticking the wads under the desks."

"Yeah," Ernesto agreed sadly. "You think I should go talk to Roxie's parents?

You know, warn them that she's in with a bad crowd?"

Paul Morales laughed. "You can do anything you want, homie. But chances are they'll cuss you out for telling horrible lies about their little angel. You know the line in that movie—'You can't handle the truth'? Most parents can't."

That night, as he tossed and turned in bed, Ernesto tried to figure out how to find out who Roxanne Torres was dating. If he got the name of that punk, then maybe he could tell the police to check out the dude for weapons.

At school the next day, Ernesto skipped lunch with his friends. He took his peanut butter and grape jelly sandwich over to a grassy place where Roxanne Torres was eating. She was picking at her yogurt alone. Her arm was still in a sling.

"How're you feeling, Roxie? Arm any better?" Ernesto asked.

"Still hurts, but it's okay," she replied. "Where's Naomi? You and her are so tight, you never hardly see one without the other." He detected a vague hurt in Roxanne's voice. Ernesto wondered whether she had liked him once, and he just never noticed because he was so wrapped up in Naomi. Ernesto knew what it was like to like someone from a distance, someone who didn't know you were alive. It was that way with Ernesto when he liked Naomi, but she only had eyes for Clay Aguirre.

Ernesto took a wild shot. "You got a hot boyfriend, Roxie." As soon as the words were out of his mouth, he took a bite of his sandwich.

Roxanne looked startled. "How do *you* know?" she demanded.

"I was driving past the Cat's Paw the other day," Ernesto explained, his mouth sticky with peanut butter and jelly. I saw you guys going in. You were hot and heavy. He's a cool-looking dude." Ernesto's heart was beginning to pound. He felt he was near to the truth.

Roxanne giggled. "Well, he *is* pretty smooth. He's not like the boys here at school. They're kinda stupid."

"I guess you're way past the boys here at Chavez," Ernesto remarked, still fishing.

"Yeah, I want a guy who can handle himself," Roxanne whined. "I don't want some little jerk who's still fighting with his parents over a curfew. I mean, give me a break."

"Are your parents okay with you dating an older guy?" Ernesto asked. "I know when my little sisters get old enough for high school, my parents are gonna be pretty strict."

"My parents work twenty-four-seven," Roxanne stated flatly. "All they got time for is work and worrying about their retirement funds. They trust me. I can take care of myself. Anyway, my guy is mega cool. He buys me things that you wouldn't believe,"

Roxanne opened her purse and showed Ernesto a cultured pearl necklace. "Isn't this awesome? My boyfriend gave me this for my eighteenth birthday. It's like worth a coupla thousand dollars. I'd never wear it at school."

Roxanne's eyes narrowed. "I suppose when Naomi turned seventeen, you bought her junk jewelry from the drugstore. I mean, that's not a cut on you. You're a kid. My boyfriend's a man."

"You're right, Roxie." Ernesto affirmed. "I couldn't afford to give Naomi something like that. I work for minimum wages. Your boyfriend must make a lot of money,"

"Yeah, he's doing good. He's really smart," Roxanne said, finishing her yogurt.

Ernesto decided to try something to catch Roxanne by surprise. "You know, I was thinking, that musta been terrible for you when that dude busted into your house the other night. You must have been scared outta your wits to see a stranger there in your living room."

Roxanne looked strange. "Yeah," she agreed. Then she added quickly, "Gotta get to class. Bye."

"Roxie, the shooting wasn't an accident was it?" Ernesto was speaking to her turned back. "Did somebody you know shoot off a gun by mistake?"

Roxanne turned. She was ashen. "*What?*" she gasped. "Why—why would you say such a thing?"

"If it was an accident, nobody would be punished, you know," Ernesto answered. "But lying about it is a crime."

Roxanne's eyes widened, as if she'd seen a ghost. "What . . . are you talking about? You're talking crazy." Roxanne stammered, "He . . . that man . . . he shot me. He came in . . . I told them. The guy . . . he shot me. An accident? What accident? I don't know what you're talking about."

Roxanne was so upset, she dropped her binder, and some papers fluttered out. When Ernesto tried to help her recover them, she screamed. "Leave me alone! How dare you say such things? Just leave me alone! You're crazy! You don't know what you're talking about!" She ran off, clutching a handful of papers and her binder. Ernesto stood watching her. She turned once and looked back at him. Then she hurried faster, as if he were chasing her, even though he was standing still.

Ernesto had no more doubt. She had lied. The whole story about the intruder coming in and shooting her was a lie. She fell to pieces when he nibbled at the edge of her false tale. She became incoherent.

Ernesto now believed Roxanne had made up the description of the nonexistent intruder. She had seen Griff Slocum standing at the twenty-four-seven store. She wanted to make up somebody unattractive and scary, and his face came to mind. Griff disgusted her when she saw him on the street. So she created the fake intruder from the image of the man she loathed.

But Ernesto had no more than dark suspicions and his gut feeling. He had nothing concrete. He had tricked Roxanne into showing her hand, but she was pretty tough. She would just be convincing in re-telling her lie if the police questioned her again. And the sad truth was that the police believed they already had their culprit in Griff Slocum. He was mentally ill, like many of the homeless in the ravine and on the streets and alleys. It was easy to believe he could do something violent. On top of that, he was facing a drug charge. The police could hold him on that while they looked for evidence that he was the shooter in both cases.

On Saturday morning, Luis Sandoval said, "Ernie, I'm driving over to the Acosta house to talk to Alex. I really feel bad about what's happening to him. He was doing good in his classes. Now he's letting this one incident ruin his whole future. He said he's thinking about dropping out of the college and maybe taking some online classes somewhere. He's talking about risking his whole future, even though his wound has healed and there's no reason he can't go back to school."

"You think he's scared or what?" Ernesto asked.

"I don't know. To tell you the truth, I can't figure it out," the father replied. "Here's a kid who graduated from Chavez High with a three-point-eight GPA. He could really go somewhere. He falls victim to a random shot, and now he's shutting down. I was wondering, Ernie, would you tag along with me? The kid might relate better to a guy close to his own age rather than an old guy like me."

"You're not an old guy, Dad," Ernesto told him.

"When I was combing my hair this morning, I spotted more gray among the black hairs, *mi hijo*," Dad responded, grinning sheepishly. "My dad used to say when the ghost threads appear in the hair, the sand is going down in the hourglass."

"Come on, Dad, you look great. You're young," Ernesto insisted. "Remember when we all went down to the beach that last hot day in summer? You looked more ripped than a lot of the young dudes. Mom was kinda put out about how the chicks were checking you out."

Dad laughed, but Ernesto could tell he enjoyed the compliment. "Well, will you come with me, Ernie?"

"Sure, Dad," Ernesto agreed. But he felt he had to tell his father what Paul had told him about Alex. And he dreaded doing that. Right now, Dad saw Alex Acosta as a fine young man who was letting irrational fear ruin his life. But there was more to it than that.

As they drove toward the Acosta house, Ernesto began to tell his father. "Dad, Paul Morales told me something about Alex that you need to know. I know the guy told the police he wasn't into gangs or drugs, but Paul has seen him using."

A pained look went through Luis Sandoval's eyes. "Oh brother!" he groaned. "I kinda suspected that a few times when he was in my class. He seemed spacey. But I thought he was just tired. Is Paul sure?"

"Yeah, Dad," Ernesto nodded yes. "He's seen Alex over at the Cat's Paw on Polk buying. Paul thinks Alex got in trouble with a dealer, couldn't pay or something, so he got shot."

Luis Sandoval shook his head sadly. "Drugs! They're a kind of terrorism, aren't they? Sucking the life from our kids before they've had a chance to live."

They pulled into the driveway of the Acosta home. Alex was home alone when he let him in. Ernesto said, "Hi." He vaguely remembered Alex as a senior last year.

"You guys want some coffee or something?" Alex asked. He seemed nervous. Earlier, Luis Sandoval had called to ask to come over. Alex wasn't enthusiastic about seeing his teacher, but he thought he should go along for looks' sake.

"Yes, thank you," Mr. Sandoval replied.

"Sugar?" Alex asked.

"No sugar in mine," Mr. Sandoval replied. Ernie held up two fingers.

Alex had made the coffee beforehand. So it took only a minute to be ready. The three now sat in the living room with their coffee.

"Alex," Mr. Sandoval began, "you have a fine record at Chavez. And you were doing well at the college, not just in my class either. You're too good to lose, Alex. Whatever problems you have, there are solutions. I'm here to help you get back on track."

The boy showed no more signs of his leg injury. He walked fine. But when he talked, he didn't look at Ernesto or his father. He looked down at the floor. "I . . . uh . . . thought I'd take some time off, get my head straight.

Lotsa guys take a year between high school graduation and college and—"

"Son," Luis Sandoval interrupted gently, "I know you have a drug problem. But that's not terminal. Good rehab can help you through that."

Alex looked up. He was pale. "I don't . . . I never . . . ," he stammered.

CHAPTER SIX

Ernesto Sandoval spoke up. "Alex, I don't know you and you don't know me. But my friends, the Ibarras, they know your folks. They tell me you're good people. Alex, you screwed up. But we all screw up one time or another. You got mixed up with some slimy dudes, and they shot you. I don't know why. Maybe you didn't pay quick enough for the poison they sold you."

Alex said nothing. He just stared at the floor. Ernesto went on.

"It's not like the end of the world, Alex. You're not the only dude our age who's used. I got friends who used and don't anymore. They're clean. They got past that, and you can too. Plenty guys got a cool gig going in their lives now. And they used drugs and put it behind them. Okay, man?"

Alex was shaking. He put the palms of his hands on his knees to steady them. "I smoked pot," he admitted. "Then I met these guys who said pot doesn't do it for you. They had something that gave a real kick. They said there's nothing like it. It was heroin."

Luis and Ernesto Sandoval listened silently to Alex's confession.

"They sold me some, and it was amazing. I wanted that feeling, and I wanted more and more. Before I knew it, I was into them for a lot. I even stole one of Mom's necklaces to pay them off, but I couldn't get enough money. After I told them that, somebody shot me. I got a call afterward. They said that was for stiffing them."

Alex buried his face in his hands. "I called my grandmother. I begged her for money to pay the dude off, and she helped me. I don't ever want to go near that stuff again. I couldn't tell my parents that I used. They're so proud of me . . ."

"Alex," Ernesto said softly, "you've got to call the police. You've got to tell them why you were shot. The gun that was used to shoot you was used to shoot a girl too. Whoever shot you probably shot her. Somebody dangerous is out there, man. You gotta come clean."

"My parents," Alex cried. "It'll kill them to know what I've been doing. They got no clue, man. I don't even know who the guy was who shot me. The shot came out of the darkness when I was jogging."

"Who sold you the heroin, son?" Ernesto's father asked.

"I don't know the guy's name," Alex responded. "He and his friends hang out at the Cat's Paw. He's a tall skinny guy, real mean. He's got earrings and a goatee."

Ernesto looked at his father. "Sounds like Cabron. You know, the other day when me and my friends got Jorge away from those bad dudes. Cabron and a guy named Simon were going to bash my brains in."

"If this Cabron and his friend packed heat," Mr. Sandoval told his son, "you guys got a lucky streak that day, Ernie. Apparently they weren't armed that day." Dad's brow creased in concern. "Or even they thought shooting you in broad daylight was too risky." Father and son locked eyes for a moment.

Mr. Sandoval turned to Alex. "Okay, just take it easy. My brother is a lawyer, and he's got a lot of friends in the police department. We'll tip off the police that they need to check out this Cabron. He may still have the gun. Just take it easy, Alex. If the gun is found on Cabron, the deal is sealed."

Mr. Sandoval spent some time urging Alex to come back to class. By the time he and Ernesto left, Alex seemed like he was ready to make a fresh start.

Back in the car, Luis Sandoval got on his cell phone with his brother. "Artie, listen. There's a creep called Cabron, hangs out at the Cat's Paw with a guy named Simon. You know the sleazy joint on Polk? We think this might be the guy who shot Alex Acosta and the girl too. I understand the same gun was used in both crimes. Well, if the police can find the gun . . ."

"Thanks, Luis," Arturo Sandoval replied. "I'll be talking to the police right away."

As they drove home, Ernesto couldn't quite put the pieces together. Was it possible that Roxanne Torres was actually dating Cabron? Did they have a fight that night? Did he try to scare her with the gun? Was he showing off? And maybe the gun went off accidentally?

Could the girl actually love Cabron so much that she'd cover for him? Why, Ernesto asked himself, would Roxanne want to cover for the dude? Was he buying her all those expensive gifts? Maybe she also feared what would happen if her parents found out whom she was dating. Dense as they were, they would freak if they knew their teenaged kid was dating a dangerous drug dealer.

When Ernesto and his father got home, Maria Sandoval was putting the finishing touches on her children's book. It was called *Don't Blink, It's a Skink*. Ernesto had spotted a blue-tailed skink one day, and that gave his mother the idea for her book. Mom was in a really happy mood. *Abuela* had entertained the girls and even watched little Alfredo. She was able to get all her work done.

"My agent is so excited," Mom enthused. "There's already buzz about the book!"

Luis Sandoval walked over and put his arms around his wife. "*Querida mia*," he whispered. "How can one woman be so beautiful and so loving and so talented, all at the same time? I am the luckiest man in the world."

Mom laughed, as Katalina and Juanita came down the hallway to join them.

Then the phone rang.

Ernesto's mother answered the phone, and immediately she looked upset. "Linda, slow down. I can't even understand what you're saying. Tell me what's happened."

Ernesto tensed up. Linda Martinez was Naomi's mother. Had something happened to Naomi? Or to someone in her family? Ernesto's heart raced, and his legs went weak.

Then his mother put the phone aside and said to her family. "The police are at the Torres house again. Linda said there are several police cars in the driveway. Mrs. Torres called Linda, and she said Roxanne is hysterical."

Mom returned to the phone. "Is there anything I can do, Linda? . . . Oh, okay. God bless you for being there for her. She must be devastated. And remember, if there's anything I can help with, just call me."

Mom closed the phone. "Linda and Naomi are going over there to help Mrs. Torres. The police are questioning Rox- anne, and I guess stuff is coming out that is just terrible. Those poor parents. Linda has such a good heart. You know, the Torres family has never been close with Linda and her family. But still she's going over there to comfort them."

"Is there anything we can do?" Dad asked.

"No. Linda said it's best if there aren't any more people there," Mom replied.

A couple of hours later, Naomi called Ernesto. He had been pacing around the house, unable to get any of his school-work done. When his cell phone rang, he snatched it.

"Ernie," Naomi said, "the police questioned Roxanne for a long time. She finally told them the truth. Her boyfriend was over, and he was showing her his gun. And it went off. That's how she got shot. The boyfriend and Roxie made up the story about the intruder to keep them both out of trouble. The boyfriend has a long rap sheet. It's that Cabron creep. You know, one of the guys who jumped you when Jorge was mixed up with the drug pushers."

"Oh man!" Ernesto groaned. "Is Roxanne in trouble?"

"Well, the police didn't take her in or anything," Naomi reported. "But, you know, she gave a false report. Sent the police on a wild goose chase. Got an innocent man arrested. Anyway, this Cabron guy is on the loose and that's bad."

Ernesto hadn't told Naomi everything about his encounter with Cabron and Simon that day. He knew it would worry her that he'd be boneheaded enough to mix it up with guys like that. Dad was right in scolding Ernesto about that move. He could have easily gotten severely injured or killed.

"I hope the cops nab the dude quick," Ernesto responded. "Hey, Naomi, you busy tomorrow?"

"I've got a lot of school stuff to do." She sounded undecided. Ernesto could hear in her tone that she was open to a suggestion.

"The weather chick said the beach would be great tomorrow," he urged. "I thought maybe in the afternoon we could go to the beach."

"I guess I could get all my stuff done tonight," Naomi said quickly. She giggled a little. "You're on, babe."

"Pick you up around one," Ernesto responded, his spirits rising. Whenever a date with Naomi was coming up, he was on top of the world. Everything else—his worries, his own projects piling up next to his computer—faded away. He was going to have time alone with Naomi.

But that night, Ernesto's thoughts turned to Cabron and Simon and what happened after the auto show. Ernesto had risked his life. And he forced his good friends to get involved in something dangerous too, just to help him. That wasn't fair to Abel, Paul, and Cruz. Still, Jorge Aguilar was now clean and back on the track team. Ernesto's bad call had ended up doing what he intended to do—save Jorge.

But what would the price have been if something had gone wrong? What if Cabron and Simon had used their guns? Maybe Ernesto Sandoval would have been lying in a satin-lined box at Our Lady of Guadalupe Church.

His bad decision was a wake-up call for Ernesto. He still wanted to save as many kids at Cesar Chavez as he could. But he wouldn't do it the way he did that Saturday afternoon. He owed himself more common sense. He owed it to his family and his friends to take better care of himself.

When Ernesto went to Bluebird Street on Sunday afternoon to pick up Naomi, he glanced across the street at the Torres home. All the blinds on the windows were drawn. It seemed as though they were grieving over there.

Naomi got into the Volvo and stared at her home through the windshield. "You know what, Ernie?" she mused. "My family has lived in this house since I was born. And before that, they lived here when my brothers were born. The Torres family moved across the street when I was about five. Roxie's almost two years older than me, but I remember us playing together a few times."

Ernesto backed out of the driveway while Naomi was speaking. "We never got close though. We went to the same elementary school, the same middle school, Chavez High. Roxie flunked some classes, so we ended up as sophomores together. Then she caught up. I guess Roxie must have had problems right along. I never figured she would hook up with a guy like Cabron. I mean, why would a girl from a nice, normal family do that?"

"Maybe her parents were too busy working to pay any attention to her," Ernesto suggested.

"Maybe," Naomi conceded. "But all families have problems. Maybe the difference is how the family feels about one another. I mean, you know how weird it's gotten at our house sometimes. But through it all, me and my brothers were the most important people in Mom and Dad's life. I never doubted that. Even when Dad is yelling and screaming at one of us, he loves us. Love is such a funny thing, Ernie. I think if you know somebody loves you, it can save you from almost anything."

They turned off the freeway onto the highway leading to the beach. In spite of the nice weather, it wasn't as crowded as Ernesto expected it to be. Ernesto and Naomi walked down to the sand and put a blanket down. "I bet the water is really cold," Naomi remarked, shivering a little.

"Let's just watch the pelicans, babe," Ernesto suggested. "If we get enough courage, we'll take a plunge."

"You know," Naomi commented, "a young guy was surfing around Santa Barbara a few weeks ago, and a shark got him. Only a hundred yards or so off the beach I think."

"I heard that," Ernesto said.

Naomi smiled. "You know what my dad did when he heard it? He slammed his fist down on the table, and all the dishes jiggled. He goes, 'Naomi, you ain't goin' swimmin' in the ocean no more. No way. The sharks are like patrolling the coastline. They're lookin' to make lunch out of anybody fool enough to go in those waters.'" Naomi had spoken her father's words in as deep a voice as she could. "So I go, 'Daddy, don't worry, I won't go swimming with the sharks.' Then he gets even madder. He tells me not to make fun of him."

Naomi turned her beautiful eyes on Ernesto and said, "Daddy is such a pain in the neck sometimes, but I love him so much. The thought of anything ever happening to him sends me into sheer terror. I want him to give me away at my wedding. I want him to play with my kids."

"*Our* kids," Ernesto said softly, hoping the wind would carry his presumptive words away.

But Naomi heard him and leaned over to kiss his cheek. Then she spoke again. "Daddy works so hard, and he doesn't take care of himself. He's overweight, and he hardly ever touches salads. Just hamburgers and tacos and enchiladas, sausages, pork chops. He gets mad at the drop of a hat. He sits there in front of the TV cursing all the people he doesn't like. And that's a lot of people."

Naomi giggled. "He hears about some brutal crime, and he wants to personally hang the culprit. He hears about those crooked politicians in that little town near LA. Remember, the ones who earned millions while the city went to the dogs? Them he wants to send to prison for life. Mom goes, 'Calm down, Felix.' But he just yells louder and says it's his constitutional right to be furious."

Ernesto laughed. "Well, your dad has given me some grief too, Naomi. When I first met him, he was telling me I was a weakling. I was a little wimp who should be playing football instead of running track. I really disliked him. I couldn't get away from there fast enough. Now that I know him better, I like the guy. I really have a lot of respect and affection for him."

Naomi looked at Ernesto with a strangely tender gaze. She seemed almost to be near tears. "You don't know how much that means to me to hear you say that. I always worried that my father would stand in our way, Ernie. It makes me so happy that you feel like that." She leaned over and hugged her boyfriend.

About fifteen minutes later, Naomi announced, "You know I'm wearing my bikini under my top and jeans— just in case. It seems to have gotten warmer, don't you think?"

"I got my swimming trunks on too, under my jeans," Ernesto responded. "I thought I'd be ready, babe, if the water was irresistible."

"Let's do it then," Naomi said, pulling off her top and giggling. "We won't go out too far."

Ernesto pulled off his T-shirt. "You don't see any dark fins, do you?" he asked.

Naomi gave him a shove. "If we see fins, we'll hightail it for the beach."

They piled their outer clothing on the blanket, and then ran, hand in hand, for the water. They splashed into the water.

"It's cold!" Naomi shrieked. "Brrrr!"

"It'll get warmer quick," Ernesto promised.

The water surged around their ankles, then their knees. When they were in to their waists Naomi squealed, "You lied!"

Ernesto howled as a wave hit him. It *was* cold.

They had swum out about twenty yards and then turned and headed back. As they came out of the water, Naomi looked at Ernesto and commented, "Oh, you are so ripped! If I wasn't so cold, I'd just stand here admiring you." The girl trotted toward the blanket. Ernesto trailed behind her, looking at the girl he loved in her blue bikini. As they dried themselves off, Ernesto said,

"Those models got nothing on you, babe. You're the hottest chick on the planet."

They sat down on the blanket and wrapped another big blanket around themselves.

"Ohhh! This is so cozy," Naomi purred. "I'm getting warmer already."

"Just looking at you, babe, makes me warm," Ernesto said, smiling. "But the blanket sure helps."

"Let's stay and watch the sun go down," Naomi suggested. "That's so special. To see it on the water."

"Yeah," Ernesto agreed.

The sky turned from pink to brilliant red.

"Oh my gosh!" Naomi sighed. "It's the most beautiful sight in the world, and it lasts just for a few minutes. Sometimes when I'm home, I'll go out and watch the sun go down. If it's really pretty, I'll stare at it until the color is all gone. I'll see people walking along, and they don't even turn their heads to look at it. I think that's sad."

"Yeah," Ernesto said. But all he was thinking was that his girl was the most beautiful sight in *his* world.

By the time the sun dropped over the horizon, their suits were dry. They got dressed and climbed the path up to where the Volvo was parked. Again on the highway, they decided to get something to eat. They stopped at a taco stand and ordered fish tacos. They were good, but not like Hortencia's. Ernesto's Aunt Hortencia ran the best taco and tamale restaurant anywhere.

"This has been such a wonderful afternoon," Naomi remarked as they walked back to the car. "Nothing spectacular, like going to a theme park, but still absolutely wonderful."

When they got on the freeway, Naomi noticed that a truck seemed to be following them. Ernesto was in the slow lane, doing no more than the speed limit. Usually a car would pass, but this one stayed behind them.

"Ernie," Naomi said with a catch in her voice, "it's probably just my imagination.

But that pickup behind us looks like it might be tailing us."

Ernesto glanced into his rearview mirror. He didn't recognize the dark Ford pickup. He couldn't see much of the driver, except it was a guy with a baseball cap. "He's probably just going in the same direction we are, Naomi."

"He's like following so close," Naomi insisted. "You'd think he'd change lanes if he wanted to go faster."

"Maybe he's gonna turn soon, so he wants to stay in this lane. Off ramp coming up," Ernesto said.

Dark thoughts went through Ernesto's mind, but he didn't want to alarm Naomi. Maybe Cabron got wind that Ernesto had sicced the police on him. Maybe he put two and two together, and now he wanted to settle a score with Ernesto.

Ernesto turned off on the Washington off ramp, and the Ford truck did the same. "We're not going down Tremayne like usual," Ernesto said in a suddenly tense voice. "We're not leading that guy to where either of us lives. I'm passing Tremayne and going on Adams. We'll turn there, see what happens."

"Okay," Naomi said. She kept glancing back at the truck, her hands clasped tightly in her lap.

Ernesto turned the Volvo off onto Adams. A large supermarket was there, and many people were coming and going. Ernesto pulled into the parking lot. If the dude in the Ford was Cabron or some other gangbanger, the place was too busy for him to try anything.

"We're parking close to the doors where there's a lot of action," Ernesto told Naomi. "Whoever the guy is, he's not likely to start trouble here."

"He's pulling in right behind us, Ernie," Naomi gasped. "Oh, I'm shaking like a leaf!" Naomi was now sure the man in the Ford had been following them. She had no more doubt of that.

Ernesto reached over and covered Naomi's hands with his. "Don't worry, babe. He's not going to try anything here. There must be fifty people walking around here. We're safe. The police station is only a block away."

The man in the baseball cap got out of the Ford and walked over to the Volvo.

CHAPTER SEVEN

It wasn't Cabron. It was a nice-looking, well-dressed young man. Ernesto didn't know him. He was standing at the driver's side window as he talked to Ernesto.

"Hi," the stranger said. "You're Ernesto Sandoval, right? I thought I recognized your Volvo back there."

"Yeah, what are you tailing us for, man?" Ernesto demanded in an unfriendly voice. He didn't like people following him, especially at night and most especially when he had precious cargo—Naomi.

"I'm sorry if I alarmed you," the man apologized. "But I spotted your Volvo coming off the beach parking. I recognized the damaged back fenders. I had seen it several times at the doughnut shop when I went there to see my girlfriend. She told me who you were—a good friend of Abel Ruiz's."

"Who are you?" Ernesto snapped, not getting out of the car.

"Victor Toro," the man answered. "The name probably has no meaning to you but—"

Ernesto made the connection then. Claudia Villa's new boyfriend. The dude Claudia dumped Abel Ruiz for. Ernesto sort of hated him right off for that. Ernesto loved Abel like a brother, and it just about broke Abel's heart when Claudia dumped him for this jerk. Claudia announced to Abel one night that she'd fallen madly in love with another guy. She loved a senior at the private boys school that was often paired with Claudia's private girls school. Poor Abel went into a serious tailspin after that.

"Oh yeah," Ernesto said crossly, "you're the dude who took up with Claudia. So what do you want with me?"

"I've heard a lot about you, Ernie, from Claudia," Victor said. "All of it good. She really likes and respects you. She says you're a warm, friendly guy, but I'm not seeing that right now."

"Well," Ernesto snarled, "consider the situation, man. I'm driving home in the dark with my chick. Suddenly I'm being tailed by this pickup truck, and I don't know who's driving it. Maybe I offended some gangbangers, and they're out to get me. Stuff like that can ruin a guy's personality, you know?"

"I just wanted a little help from someone who knows Claudia," Victor Toro said. "When she was dating Abel Ruiz, I suppose you saw a lot of her."

"Yeah, okay," Ernesto replied.

"She's a wonderful girl," Toro said. "I really like her. But she's into this relationship more than me, you see. I mean, I came into the doughnut shop a few times. Then we met again at this dance, and the girl freaked. Not that I didn't enjoy our time together and all that, but it was getting too intense. The bottom line is that, well, Claudia went nuts for me, and I don't feel the same way. To be blunt, I'm kinda looking for an exit, and I thought you might have some advice on how best to handle it."

Ernesto looked over at Naomi in disbelief. Then he returned his attention to the young man. Ernesto had never liked Victor Toro, and he was liking him even less as the moments went by.

"So, let me get this straight," Ernesto said. "You let the chick fall for you and led her to believe you guys had something going. So she dumped a guy who loved her with all his heart. You enjoyed the fun times, but now she's crimping your style. Now you're looking to dump her like she dumped Abel *for you*. Is that what you're saying, man? Give it to me straight. I'm not a complicated guy, but this is blowing my mind, dude."

"You make me sound like some kind of a jerk—or worse," Victor Toro complained.

"All I'm asking is how to let her down as easily as possible and I thought—"

"Oh hey," Ernesto interrupted. Ernesto's voice was low and bitter. "Excuse me for making you sound like a jerk, Toro. Why would I do that? Just because you ruined a real good relationship between my best friend and a girl he really loved. And all the while you didn't care at all for her."

"That's not fair, man," Toro whined. "I hoped we might grow closer, but she's not my type. I'm just asking for a clue on how to let her down easy. Since you know her, I thought . . . I mean . . . I'm trying to do the right thing here. I hate seeing the chick just hanging in the wind crying her eyes out."

"Oh yeah, now I get it," Ernesto exclaimed bitterly. "Maybe I could go tell Abel that now that Mr. Wonderful has dumped Claudia. Maybe he could catch her as she falls. It's not like Abel has any pride. No way. You want off the hook. You don't want to be the bad guy, preppy boy. So you

128

toss Claudia into the garbage. Abel grabs her and takes her back."

"You're being pretty rotten about all this, Sandoval," Victor Toro stated indignantly. "I guess I had you all wrong. You're an ugly–tempered guy, and I'm sorry I bothered you."

"I'm a lot sorrier than you, Toro!" Ernesto yelled at the man as he walked away.

Naomi whistled. "Ernie! I've never seen you like that!" she gasped.

Ernesto took a deep breath. He was usually polite and gracious even in touchy situations. It took a lot to make him lose his cool. But he had gone through so many weeks of seeing his best friend, Abel Ruiz, suffer over losing Claudia. Abel had never had a close girlfriend until he met Claudia. He poured his heart and soul into pleasing her. He was never so happy as when he was with her. To watch his big, good heart break into pieces like shards of glass tore Ernesto up. Now, to think that Claudia had dumped Abel for some shallow creep who was throwing her away like a used tissue. Victor Toro knew Claudia had a steady guy. Why did he move in on her? Claudia and Abel were doing fine.

Ernesto moved in on Naomi while she was still dating Clay Aguirre. But that was different. Ernesto had fallen in love with Naomi almost at first sight. Even so, if she and Clay had had a good relationship, he would have stayed away. But Clay had been treating Naomi like trash, and finally he struck her. Otherwise, Ernesto would never have tried to win Naomi away from a good guy whom she loved and who loved her.

"I guess tonight wasn't my proudest moment," Ernesto admitted. "But she hurt Abel *so bad* and for a creep like Toro!"

"I understand," Naomi admitted. "I love a lot of things about you, Ernie. But one of the big things is your loyalty to anyone you care about. I do understand. I know how close you are to Abel. But what are you going to do now?"

"I'll have to tell Abel. He has a right to know," Ernesto replied. "I don't know how he feels about Claudia right now. He doesn't talk about her anymore, and I don't bring her up. Maybe he hates her for what she did to him, but I don't think so. Abel can't hate. I'm much better at hating than he is. Abel's dating Bianca now, but he told me they're just friends. He said he didn't want a real girlfriend until he's older. He told me he doesn't want anything ever again to hurt as much as losing Claudia hurt. But I've got to tell him."

Ernesto drove first to Bluebird Street to drop Naomi home. He never just stopped and let her out. He always walked her to the door and even went inside for a few minutes. He felt he owed that to Naomi and her parents. Naomi was his precious girlfriend, but, long before that, she was her parents' precious child.

Felix Martinez was still up, sitting in his favorite chair watching television. "Hey, Naomi, Ernie," he yelled. "What'd I tell you about that girl across the street? She was lyin' through her teeth right along. Was on the news. Whole story was a lie. Little creep. Made all that trouble for that poor homeless dude like he doesn't have a hard enough row to hoe. They ought to get her one of those striped suits and lock her up for a while."

"Anything about the police catching Cabron on the news?" Ernesto asked Mr. Martinez.

Naomi's father shook his head no. "He probably skipped town. But I did hear about that guy . . ." Mr. Martinez snapped his fingers in the air.

"Griff Slocum?" Ernesto supplied.

"Yeah," Mr. Martinez said, "that's the one. They sent 'im to a rehab center for his drug problem. But he'll only be there a few days. He's off the hook for the shooting. He'll be back on the street before long. The county don't have the money to baby-sit him for long."

Naomi put her hands on Ernesto's shoulders, pulling him down a little and then she kissed him on the lips. "Goodnight, babe," she whispered.

"Goodnight, *mi querida dulce,*" Ernesto said, kissing her back.

"*Ayyy!*" Felix Martinez laughed. "Hot time in the old town tonight."

Ernesto laughed. "Goodnight, Mr. Martinez," he said before he left.

Ernesto was still stunned by what Victor Toro had done. He didn't know quite how to handle it. He was tempted to call Paul Morales and see what he thought, but that would be disrespecting Abel. Abel deserved to hear it straight from Ernesto and not secondhand. Then it'll be up to Abel to decide whom to share it with.

Ernesto felt he knew Abel probably better than anyone else. But he wasn't sure how Abel would handle the information. Ernesto thought Abel would likely be shocked and then feel humiliated. Claudia had dumped Abel for someone who was trivial and worthless. Ernesto didn't even want to think about how that would affect

133

Abel. Could Abel possibly want to go and comfort Claudia? Could he even take her back, assuming that she would want to go back with him?

Later, lying awake in his bed, Ernesto worried half the night over what to say to Abel. He finally decided he'd catch Abel early Monday morning and be matter-of-fact about it. No way was he going to tell Abel that Victor Toro was dumping Claudia. That would make Abel think his girlfriend had chosen a total jerk over him. Ernesto decided to make it sound as though Victor and Claudia had just agreed to split. That would save Abel's pride.

"Hey, Abel!" Ernesto called to him early Monday morning as he came walking to class.

"Hey, Ernie. Cops get Cabron yet?" Abel asked.

"Nothing so far," Ernesto shook his head no. "He's got serious charges against him. Shooting Roxie was accidental, but he meant to shoot Alex Acosta. That bullet was a collection notice."

"Yeah," Abel agreed, "we had a close call that day coming from the auto show."

"You said it, man," Ernesto said. "Fool that I am, I put all you guys in danger." He was breathing hard, uneasy about what he had to say. "Hey, I ran into that guy Victor Toro the other night."

Abel's eyes widened. The pain was still there.

"He and Claudia aren't together anymore," Ernesto said.

"He tell you that?" Abel asked.

"Yeah," Ernesto responded, "we just ran into each other at the supermarket. I asked about Claudia, and he goes, 'We don't see each other anymore.' He seems like a jerk, Abel."

Abel didn't say anything. Ernesto couldn't figure by the look on his friend's face what he was thinking.

135

"Well," Ernesto said, "gotta get to AP History. Bustos comes down really hard if you're late. The guy takes no prisoners."

Abel nodded without saying a word and walked on. He seemed very deep in thought. Ernesto hoped the guy wouldn't take up with Claudia again. He'd been hurt enough on that road. Ernesto figured Claudia had to be a flake to fall head over heels in love with a jerk like Toro when she was dating a great guy like Abel.

There was track practice in the afternoon, and Ernesto was relieved to see Jorge Aguilar warming up. Most of the guys from last year were still on the team. Julio Avila, Eddie Gonzales, and Ernesto.

Rod Garcia was new on the team. Ernesto thought Garcia joined the team hoping he could beat Ernesto at *something*. Even in AP History, Garcia was breaking his neck to do better than Ernesto. You got points for participation in that class, and Garcia's hand was up *all* the time. It got so that Mr. Bustos had to ask him to allow other students to participate.

Coach Muñoz timed the boys. Ernesto was humbled to discover that Julio Avila came in first, Rod Garcia came in second, and he was a poor third.

"You need to do more running, Ernie," Coach Muñoz advised with disappointment on his face. "We rely on you in the relay, and you've lost a step."

Last year, Ernesto often ran ten miles a day. This year he was a lot busier with AP History, his after-school jobs, and functions as the senior class president. He found it hard to fit in running time. Then Alex Acosta got shot, and everyone thought there was a random shooter in the *barrio*. After that, running at night was out. His parents didn't want Ernesto running to and from work, as he liked to do. Ernesto wished the police would find Cabron. Then he could go back to running in the dark and getting back his speed and endurance.

When Ernesto ran to school and to work, he saved on gas too. The Volvo was reliable, but it guzzled pricey gas. It cost Ernesto money he didn't have to spare. He was saving every penny he could for college and law school. He didn't want to graduate with a staggering college loan debt, and his parents were in no position to pay his way. Three younger siblings were right behind him.

"Boy, Sandoval," Rod Garcia taunted him after practice, "you really lost your edge."

"I can get it back," Ernesto countered. But Ernesto was not sure how he would do that.

"You hate to lose at anything, don't you?" Garcia asked.

"I guess that's true," Ernesto admitted. "I know I can't be first in everything. But I can do a lot better than I did today, and I intend to improve. Like they say, if you shoot for the moon, you might not make it, but at least you'll clear the trees. If you don't shoot for the moon, you won't even get out of the woods."

Later that day, when Ernesto got home from school, Mom was still glowing over the completion of her book.

"My agent said my book might be chosen by the science association that selects books for primary grades," Maria Sandoval announced. "That would be such an honor." She smiled at Ernesto. "It'd increase my royalties too, and I could help you with college. You wouldn't have to pay it all."

"It's okay, Mom," Ernesto assured her. "Don't worry about that."

"Still," Mom giggled, "it wouldn't hurt having a best-selling author for a mother. I mean, I still can't believe it. I've been to book fairs, and readers want to pose for pictures with me! I keep pinching myself, thinking, 'Is this really happening to little old Maria Vasquez Sandoval?'"

"Yeah, Mom," Ernesto grinned. "And then your mom'll get a charge out of your success too. She wanted you to be a big CEO or something, but a published author is lots more cool than that."

Ernesto walked over to give his mother a hug. "I'm proud of you, Mom, but not just because of the books. It's because of who you have always been—a really awesome mom," he told her.

Right about then, Luis Sandoval got home from Cesar Chavez High. He came in the house listening to the news on his iPhone. "There's a police standoff on Polk," he reported. "They've cordoned off the cross streets and evacuated two apartments." Dad's voice was tense.

"What's going down?" Ernesto asked.

"Somebody holed up in an apartment over there," Dad answered. "The police have the place surrounded, and they might be getting a SWAT team. It's likely to be a gang thing. Lotsa gang activity over on Polk. They conduct sweeps, and it's good for a little while. Then they all come back, and it's like nothing happened."

Ernesto's cell phone rang. It was Naomi, who was at home. "Ernie, the police are across the street at the Torres house. My mom is over there with Mr. and Mrs. Torres. They're out of their minds with worry. They had a big fight with Roxanne last night. She ran out the door, and they haven't seen her since ten last night. They think she got a text from Cabron and she ran away with him."

Naomi's voice was shaking. "You know about the trouble over on Polk? I think the police may have cornered Cabron there . . . Oh, Ernie, it's possible that Roxie's holed up with him."

"Oh man!" Ernesto groaned. "I didn't think even Roxie would be that stupid. Throwing in with a dude who's wanted in a shooting! I mean, he shot Alex Acosta. That's a felony. What was she thinking?"

Roxanne's face flashed before Ernesto's mind. He didn't even know her until the middle of his junior year at Chavez. He hadn't known any of the juniors. When he did see her a few times on campus, he didn't pay any attention to her. Ernesto was always too busy trying to win over Naomi Martinez from that creep Clay Aguirre. Ernesto was too busy falling in love with Naomi to even notice another girl.

Ernesto never even knew, until just a few days ago, that maybe Roxanne Torres had had a crush on him. While he was ignoring her, she was looking at him, an interesting new guy who'd just arrived from Los Angeles.

Roxanne was a pretty girl, but she always seemed to end up with loser boyfriends. She gossiped a lot, and she was cruel sometimes. She liked to post embarrassing incidents about other students online. But she wasn't really a bad girl. Ernesto didn't think she used drugs. She was just a kid who made bad choices most of the time.

"Poor Cathy and Jamie Torres!" Mom groaned at the news. "Roxie is their only child . . ."

Ernesto figured Cabron was the worst bad choice of all.

CHAPTER EIGHT

The Sandoval family sat watching television updates of the standoff on Polk Street. The SWAT team had arrived.

"Is somebody gonna get shot?" Katalina asked, wide-eyed. "Look at all the soldiers." To the child, the heavily armed police officers looked like soldiers.

"We hope not," Luis Sandoval responded, putting his arm around his daughter's shoulders. "The SWAT team is really efficient. They do everything possible to take people out safely."

"You gotta appreciate the terrible job those cops have, though," Ernesto remarked, shaking his head. "In a way, it's as dangerous as a battlefield. Like a couple weeks ago, thirteen police officers were shot all around the country. A couple of them were killed. It's so awful."

"I wonder if that Cabron has any family around here," Maria Sandoval said. "Sometimes they can get a family member to talk someone out in a situation like this."

"He seemed really hardcore, Mom," Ernesto replied. "Probably his family has given up on him a long time ago—if he ever had a family, that is. Lotsa kids in the *barrio* been kicked around from foster home to foster home, like Paul Morales. It's a miracle that dude turned out so good."

"I'm scared," Juanita interjected. "Those bad men won't come here, will they?"

Maria Sandoval put her arms around her youngest daughter and assured her. "Don't worry, honey. The police have the apartment surrounded, and the bad people can't get out. It's happening way over on Polk Street too. They won't bother us here on our street."

144

Ernesto stared at the screen and spoke to no one in particular. "A few days ago at school I talked to Roxanne. She was bragging about the expensive gift Cabron gave her for her birthday. Real good cultured pearls. Several thousand bucks. I didn't know at the time that Cabron was her boyfriend. But I thought any dude who could buy that for a chick had to be on the wrong side of the law."

"Something happened," Dad noted. "Lot of police action."

"Oh thank God!" Mom cried. "They're bringing them out. It seems to be over, and nobody was hurt."

"That girl is crying," Katalina said. "Do you see? That's Roxanne from Naomi's street, and she's crying."

"Yes, I see," Mom acknowledged.

Cabron was in handcuffs. He hung his head down, and you could barely make him out. Ernesto recognized the slender build and the wispy goatee. A chill went through Ernesto's body. This is the dude who might've killed him that Saturday.

"I'm so glad it's over," Maria Sandoval declared. "And it could have been so much worse. It could have been a tragedy."

"I guess it was just Cabron and Roxie holed up in the apartment," Luis Sandoval said. "The poor child. Only eighteen and she's in so much trouble. It was bad enough how she lied about being shot, but to be barricaded in the apartment with a felon . . ."

"Will they get her a lawyer?" Ernesto asked.

"I imagine her parents will," Dad answered. "They're not rich, but they both work and have money. Otherwise she'll have a public defender. I think I'll give Arturo a ring. He knows about this situation. He might contact the girl's parents and be able to give them good advice on what to do next."

Ernesto thought about Arturo Sandoval, his uncle, *abogado del barrio*. He'd finished law school at the top of his class.

He had offers from two major law firms in Los Angeles to join their practice. But he chose to stay in the *barrio* where he grew up. "These are my people, and I want to be here for them," he once stated. Uncle Arturo made good money as a lawyer but not nearly as much as he might make in Los Angeles. He often worked *pro bono*, asking no money at all for people in need who could not afford a lawyer. Ernesto admired him so much. Uncle Arturo was a big reason Ernesto wanted to be a lawyer too. He wanted to be the kind of lawyer his uncle was.

During the next week at Chavez High, Ernesto noticed that Abel Ruiz was unusually quiet. He never talked a lot, but now he said almost nothing. He went to work at the Sting Ray, and he was making good grades, so he had to be studying. But he seemed deep in thought whenever Ernesto ran into him.

Ernesto didn't want to ask Abel, but he thought Abel's behavior had a lot to do

with Claudia Villa. Abel was trying to figure out what to do. He was probably wondering whether Claudia was having second
thoughts about dumping him. Maybe she
was hoping against hope that they could
get together again. That made Ernesto feel
guilty. He now thought he shouldn't have
censored what Victor Toro had said. What
if Abel knew that Toro dumped Claudia?
What if he knew that otherwise she'd still
be with him? Knowing all that could influ-
ence Abel's decision.

Ernesto thought he should have given
Abel the blunt truth and not have tried to
spare his feelings.

Later in the week, Ernesto was working at Hortencia's place. Paul Morales and
Carmen Ibarra came in and ordered shrimp
tacos. "Ernie," Paul said, "my brother's
getting out next month. David's getting
paroled."

Ernesto knew Paul was living for the
day his brother left prison. Even though
they grew up for most of their childhoods in

different foster homes, they were very close. They strove to get together as much as they could. David was the only family Paul had. Sometimes Paul talked about his brother moving back with him in his apartment and getting his life back on track. Whenever he did, Paul's eyes sparkled brightly.

Ernesto glanced at Carmen. He wondered how she felt deep down. Her parents weren't thrilled that she was dating Paul Morales. Now that his ex-con brother was in the mix, it had to be more challenging for her. But Carmen was smiling cheerfully as she ate her taco.

"I've met David already," Carmen said. "Paul took me up the prison twice. He's a nice guy. He's different from Paul, but you can see that they're brothers. I mean, they're both good-looking. But, of course, nobody is as hot as Paul."

Paul smiled and winked at Ernesto. Carmen went on.

"David is more quiet. Maybe that's because he's had a rough time of it. I mean,

149

it can't be easy living in a prison. I'm not saying he's some kind of an angel. But it must be hard to live with all those bad guys when deep down you're a good guy who just made some bad mistakes.

"Actually," Carmen said, "Paul has rented a bigger apartment right down the hall from where he lived. I'm helping him fix it up so the guys have some privacy. It's easy to divide this bigger room with one of those room dividers. Our big project now is getting David a job. People are really kinda prejudiced against hiring guys who've been in prison. I told Daddy, and he's going to ask around. I mean, when you're a councilman like Daddy, you know everybody. He'll spread the word."

"Eat your taco, babe," Paul said.

"Dude," Paul turned to Ernesto. "I was driving around with Cruz and Beto, and I saw that clown Victor Toro. You know, the one who stole Abel's chick. He was going by in his truck, and there was some red-haired chick with him. I thought at first it was Claudia wearing a red wig. Then the chick turned her head, and she wasn't such a looker, if you get my meaning. What's with that? You know anything about it, Ernie?"

Ernesto hesitated before saying, "He broke up with Claudia."

"*What*?" Paul gasped. "What's with that? They've been together a few weeks, man. Her idea or his?"

"Uh . . . well," Ernesto replied, "I told Abel they just split up. But the truth is, the dude wanted out."

"Oh man!" Paul sighed. "Claudia got dumped like she dumped Abel. What goes around comes around. I like Claudia when we all worked at the doughnut shop. She was a nice chick. I was real happy when she and Abel got together. Abel's a real good friend of mine and a darn nice dude. He's been there for me more than once and I got his back too. I always thought, though, that Claudia was gullible. This Toro jerk must've come on strong and swept her away. Got her to ditch Abel, maybe the best guy she'll ever know. Now the jerk dumped her? I'd like to shove his head through a wall."

"That wouldn't do any good," Ernesto said. He really liked Paul, but he was always a little nervous around him too. When he was angry, there was no telling what he might do.

"Ernie," Paul asked, "you think Abel would be dumb enough to take Claudia back?"

"Come on, Paul," Carmen chimed in, "that wouldn't necessarily be dumb. Maybe Claudia just made a mistake in a weak moment. She's a kid. Maybe she got a stupid crush on this Toro guy. She just forgot for a little while what Abel really meant to her. I mean, even if you love somebody, you can get knocked off the tracks by some silly infatuation."

"You better never get knocked off the tracks, babe," Paul commanded, with a smile on his lips, but darkness in his eyes. "I'd have to take him out to the Mojave Desert and stake him to an anthill."

Carmen washed her fish taco down with a ginger ale. Then she spoke. "You see what I have to put up with, Ernie? He's a crazy, wild madman. But here I am, still hopelessly in love with him as if he were a nice normal person."

Paul threw his arm around Carmen's shoulders and kissed her full on the mouth. "This chick is so hot I don't even mind kissing her while her lips still taste like shrimp."

Paul looked at Ernesto again. "Poor Abel, I called him the other night. I asked him if he'd wanna go to the monster truck rally with me and Cruz. But he said he was tired or something. He's always *loved* the monster truck rally. I bet he was stewing about what to do about that little rat, Claudia. I need to go over to Abel's house and straighten him out."

"I'm sure Abel's mother will be glad to see you," Carmen noted dryly.

"Listen to her," Paul wisecracked. "She's acting like I'm not welcome in nice homes like the Ruiz residence."

153

"Mrs. Ruiz won't want to see you. But poor Mr. Ruiz is so henpecked he has no opinion about anything," Carmen said.

"Penelope likes me though," Paul insisted, beaming. "To that little chick I'm a superhero. She likes my snake tattoo almost as much as your sisters do, Ernie. I look after her like she's my own little sister. Abel's kid sister is *my* kid sister. Nothing bad is ever gonna happen to her. That's why me and Cruz and Beto cornered that rat Max Costa who was trying to mess with little Penelope. We terrorized the creep out of his wits."

"Paul, I don't want to hear that stuff," Carmen demanded. She looked at Ernesto, "Did he ever tell you what they did?"

"Sort of," Ernesto replied.

"We jumped him," Paul explained with a scary amount of glee. "Then we pushed him against the wall and tickled his Adam's apple with the tip of a switchblade. He turned as white as a stone. You can bet he's not going on Facebook no more and trolling for little fourteen-year-old girls. Yeah, I took care of business for my friend."

"Paul, what could you tell Abel that would help him?" Ernesto asked. "I don't even know what he should do."

"He just needs to know I'm there for him," Paul answered, getting off the stool at the counter.

"He knows that, Paul," Ernesto said. "I now you're here for me too. I'll always know that. I think I might be dead or in the hospital right now if not for you and Abel and Cruz. You guys got me out of a tight spot that Saturday we rescued Jorge from the gangbangers."

Carmen turned sharply. "What are you talking about?" she demanded.

"Oh," Paul said, "I forgot to tell you, babe. Paul told Carmen all about their scrape with the gangbangers.

"My gosh!" Carmen groaned. "You guys were in a fight with somebody like Cabron! The guy it took the SWAT team to corner over on Polk?"

Paul laughed. "He's really a coward, babe. I knew he'd come out of that apartment as meek as a lamb. He can hide in the shadows and shoot Alex Acosta in the leg over an unpaid bill. But he's chicken when he sees dudes like us."

By now, Hortencia was ready to close the shop. As Paul, Ernesto, and Carmen left Hortencia's, Carmen turned to Ernesto and said, "Wish me luck, Ernie."

Paul roared with laughter. He threw his arm around Carmen, pulling her against him and kissing her. She giggled helplessly. Ernesto could not remember a time he saw Paul Morales so happy. He knew it had to do with the love and support Carmen gave him unconditionally. But also, his brother was coming home. Finally, his brother was coming home.

Right before the trio went out the door, Hortencia hailed Ernesto. Paul and Carmen went on alone while Ernesto talked to his *Tía* Hortencia.

"He's quite a character, Ernie," she commented. "Somehow it's hard to imagine you guys are friends."

Ernesto laughed. "I hear you. But the fact is you couldn't have a better friend in the world than Paul Morales if you're in trouble. He wouldn't just go a little ways for you. He'd go the distance. Not many dudes would do that. Some people go a lifetime without getting real friends. I'm lucky. I got Abel Ruiz and Paul Morales. They're as close as brothers to me."

Hortencia shook her head. "I've met Councilman Ibarra, Carmen's father. Wonderful, colorful man. He's done so much for the *barrio*. Mr. Ibarra has revitalized all the programs that help the people. He's helping the homeless and people needing jobs. He got the Nicolo Sena Scholarship program funded again for needy high school grads going to college. But I'm trying to picture Carmen Ibarra and Paul Morales as a match . . ."

Ernesto laughed again. "Oh, it's interesting all right. But Mr. Ibarra loves Carmen so much that he's accepted Paul as best he can. Carmen is a strong girl. You can't manipulate her. She knows what she wants. She loves Paul, rattlesnake tattoo and all."

"Well," Hortencia admitted, "love is amazing. I'm in my thirties, and I was very happy to be single. I am my own woman. I never wanted to get involved with a man and do the marriage thing. My freedom is so important to me. But then I met Oscar Perez. I listened to his Latin band and looked at him, and I lost my mind. And in the springtime I am giving up all I cherish—my freedom, my independence—all for Oscar who makes me crazy when I am in his arms."

Ernesto knew Hortencia loved Oscar Perez. But her words made him doubt she was happy about being married. Hortencia looked directly at her nephew and spoke.

"We are fools for love, Ernesto. You will see me in Our Lady of Guadalupe

Church in one of those impossible frilly white dresses. I always laughed at them. I will be looking into the dark eyes of this man I am insane over, promising to love, honor, and whatever . . . I will say anything. Until death do us part. I believe that."

"I'm happy for you, *Tía*," Ernesto told her. "I'll be there at the wedding, you may be sure of that. You have always been beautiful, *Tía*, but since you're in love you are radiant. There's a special glow."

"Ernesto," Hortencia explained, "the reason I hailed you today was, I overheard the talk at your end of the counter. I knew it was your quitting time, and I stopped you from leaving with your friends because I want to tell you something. In a few weeks, I'll be hiring another counterman Harry is quitting. I would like to hire some nice reliable person, and I have several in mind. But for you, *mi sobriño favorito*, I would hire your friend's brother. I know how hard it will be for the young man to get his first job out of prison, and I would do that for you."

"*Tía*," Ernesto gasped, his voice full of emotion, "that is so kind of you." Hortencia was always Ernesto's favorite aunt among all his father's brothers and sisters. He felt close to Uncle Arturo too, but Hortencia was so warm and lovable. When Ernesto lived with his family in Los Angeles, she visited often. She would take Ernesto to the theme parks, and those days held a magical place in Ernesto's memory.

"Well," Hortencia declared, "you tell your friend Paul. He should tell his brother to see if he can find a better job somewhere else. I mean, a counterman is not a wonderful job. But if he runs into too many closed doors, he can have a job here. He can get his foot in the door of the working life outside the prison. I would do it for you, Ernie, because your friend Paul means so much to you."

Tía Hortencia placed her hand on Ernesto's shoulder. "When we Sandoval kids were growing up, Ernie, your father was my special friend. Luis was my protector.

I loved all my siblings, but he was always special. You are much like him, Ernie. You are always trying to help the underdog. If anybody messed with little Hortencia— and, yes, I was a runt—they had Luis to deal with. I always felt well protected because Luis was strong and well respected."

Ernesto thanked his aunt again, and they said goodnight. Ernesto had jogged to work now that Cabron was behind bars and no longer a threat in the *barrio*. Now he jogged toward home. He went down Washington Street, then turned on Tremayne. It wasn't far to his house on Wren Street.

It felt great to be running again. Ernesto could feel strength returning to his legs. He knew his muscles would ache tomorrow, but it would be good pain. He kept going over and over Hortencia's gesture in his mind, and he smiled. A misting rain had begun to fall. It felt good against Ernesto's face. He felt a lot better jogging, even with the rain in his face, than sitting behind the wheel of the Volvo.

CHAPTER NINE

When Ernesto got in, his father was in the living room watching the ten o'clock news on TV. He turned off the TV and smiled at his son. "You're wet, *mi hijo*," he noted.

"Just a little," Ernesto replied, shaking the raindrops from his thick hair. "Anything important on the news?"

"Well," Dad answered, "the old planet is still rotating around the sun even though we haven't solved many of our problems. How did it go at the tamale shop tonight?"

"It was good, Dad. I like working there. Just about all the customers are friends of Hortencia's," Ernesto said.

"My sister has always been popular. When we were kids in our little house, it was always crammed with Hortencia's friends," Luis Sandoval said.

"You know what she told me tonight, Dad?" Ernesto asked. "She said you were her favorite sibling. You were her protector."

Dad laughed. "Well, she was always small. Five foot two, hardly a hundred pounds. The boys liked her, and sometimes I had to make sure they didn't step over the line."

"Something else too, Dad," Ernesto added. "Paul Morales's brother, David, is getting out of prison soon, and he'll be looking for a job. Carmen and Paul came in Hortencia's tonight. *Tía* overheard us talking about how tough it is for someone just out of prison to get a job. She told me that because Paul is my friend, if David can't get anything else, he has a job at her tamale shop as a counterman. That blew me away, Dad. I mean, I've always loved *Tía* Hortencia, but to think she'd make an offer like that is just amazing. I was like speechless.

It was out of left field. I never expected something like that."

"Yeah," Luis Sandoval said, "that sounds like my sister. When we were kids, there were latchkey kids in the *barrio*. She'd find out that they'd be coming home to an empty house. So here would come Hortencia with like four little kids. She'd bring them home like a kind of Pied Piper. And Mama, being Mama, she'd put out snacks for everybody. It seemed like we always had strange kids munching down afternoon snacks in our house."

Dad's face turned serious then. "What was David in prison for, Ernie? You might have told me before, but . . ."

"Paul never gave me many details, Dad. He just said vague things, like that David liked nice stuff and needed it more than Paul did. They both grew up in foster homes, separated for most of their childhood. Paul told me David was arrested for burglary. I'm not sure if it was a one-time thing or if he did it often. One thing, though, Paul said his brother is not violent. He never even came close to hurting anybody."

"He's older than Paul, isn't he?" Dad asked.

"Yeah, Paul is twenty now, and David's almost twenty-three," Ernesto answered. "Carmen said she's gone to the prison to visit David. She said he's a pretty nice guy. Quieter than Paul."

"Carmen is so in love with Paul Morales that she'd put the best spin on the brother no matter what," Dad suggested. "Poor Emilio Ibarra, he still can't get over the prospect of having Paul in the family. Emilio was dreaming of Carmen falling for some nice, charming sort of nerdy guy. You know, someone like Carmen's sister married, Ivan Redondo."

Ernesto chuckled. "Poor Ivan is such a nerd, but Lourdes loves him. Don't get me wrong, I like Ivan. He's a good guy. He goes to the prison and teaches Bible class to the men there. Paul couldn't stand Ivan. Then one day he got stuck driving Ivan to a birthday party at the Ibarra house. During the ride, Ivan started telling Paul how he'd been bullied all his life, and Paul started feeling sorry for the guy. To top it all off, it turned out that Ivan had David Morales in his Bible class. He knew all along that Paul's brother was in prison—before any of us knew—and he never said a word. Paul was really touched by that. Ever since then, you don't say anything bad about Ivan Redondo around Paul."

"Well, that says something about David's and Paul's character," Dad commented, "and Ivan's as well."

"Yeah," Ernesto agreed. "You know, Paul has been living in that little studio apartment, but now his landlady let him rent a bigger place. It's got this nice big bedroom. They're gonna divide it into two small bedrooms so both guys got some privacy. Some of us are going over there on the weekend to help fix things up. Abel, Cruz, and Beto are coming, and I'm going too. When Ivan found out, he said he was coming too. I thought that was pretty cool."

On Saturday morning, a caravan of vehicles headed down Cardinal Street, led by Cruz's van. Ernesto was driving his Volvo, and Abel was in his Jetta. Bringing up the rear was Ivan Redondo in a pickup truck, something he didn't usually drive.

Ivan Redondo was usually in a white shirt and dressy navy pants, but now he wore a T-shirt and jeans, as everybody else did. However, their T-shirts and jeans looked rattier.

"Here comes the U.S. Cavalry," Paul Morales declared as the five boys came into the apartment. Ernesto and Abel went to work putting up the room divider, which was a bookcase with shallow shelves. Paul's single bed had been in the middle of the large bedroom, along with a chest of drawers. What would be David's bedroom was empty except for a chair.

"I'm gonna get a bed and a chest of drawers on Monday," Paul explained. "There's a furniture store on Washington sells stuff real cheap."

"You can get it even cheaper at the thrift store," Cruz suggested.

"I can spring for new stuff," Paul said.

"That's good," Ivan agreed. "I don't like the idea of used beds. You can have a lot of problems." A look of extreme distaste came over his face. "Like bedbugs!"

"Yeah," Beto added, "but beggars can't be choosers. My folks get a lot of used stuff. New furniture costs a fortune."

"You got it right," Abel said. "My parents just got a new bed—I mean, a really good one. It's the kind where you set the kind of firmness you want, and it can be different on each side. It cost over a thousand dollars. Lotsa people pay even more."

"Yes," Ivan said, looking apologetic. "My parents just got new furniture for the whole house. Brand new bedroom sets in every room, even the guest rooms. They have three guest rooms. One of them has this nice new single bed and a little chest of drawers with a mirror. We never have that many guests. The room is going to sit empty. I told my mom I needed the stuff from that bedroom."

Paul stared at Ivan. The other boys, smiling at one another, knew what was coming.

"What are you saying, man?" Paul finally asked.

"It's in the pickup," Ivan explained, still looking strangely apologetic.

The Redondos lived atop a lovely canyon where all the houses were huge. Most had Olympic-sized swimming pools. The backyards were filled with expensive sculptures, with water pouring from the mouths of leaping porpoises. Ivan had never been popular with the rich kids at his school. He was tall and skinny and kind of homely, and he hated rock music and loved opera. Now that Ivan was married to Lourdes Ibarra, he was mixing with a whole other group of young people. Most of them were poor or lower middle class, and he felt guilty that he had so much.

"*What's* in the pickup, dude?" Paul asked.

"The bed and the chest of drawers," Ivan replied sheepishly. "Maybe Ernesto would help me carry it in." The other guys in room snickered.

"*You brought a bed*?" Paul asked, disbelief on his face. "And a chest of drawers?"

"Yes," Ivan answered. "The bed has never been slept in. I told Mom it was a sin to put a nice new bed in a guest room we never used. Mom agreed right away. Mom is always on my side. Dad said I'm a fool. He says that all the time. I think it's because he played football in college, and I was on the school chess team."

Ernesto, Paul, and Ivan went to the pickup truck and saw a beautiful new bed and a walnut chest of drawers.

"I could get you one too," Ivan offered. "Would you like a new bed, Paul?"

"This ain't happening," Paul mumbled, shaking his head in disbelief.

"It would be nicer than the bed you're using, Paul," Ivan noted as they carried the furniture into the apartment.

"No, no, no!" Paul protested. "I like my bed. Dude, I mean, I don't know what to say. I didn't expect you'd do this. I never thought you'd do this. I owe you one, Ivan. You told me about your neighbors up there on the hill. You know, the ones who throw pumpkins at you when you're playing your opera music. You know those guys? Well, I'll come up there and punch their lights out for you if you want. I'll do it for you, Ivan."

Ivan started to laugh. Then Ernesto, Abel, and even Cruz and Beto joined in. Ernesto hadn't seen Abel laugh so hard in a very long time.

Paul walked over then and gave Ivan a bear hug. Ernesto couldn't swear to it, and he wouldn't have dared mentioned it, but he was sure Paul's eyes looked a little teary.

The boys worked for several hours. When they were done, everything was ready for David. The apartment looked perfect after Ernesto and Abel did some much needed cleaning. When all the work was done, they sent out for pepperoni pizza, pineapple-topped pizza, and double cheese pizza. The boys washed it all down with sodas. After a busy day, Paul thanked all his friends, and they all headed out.

Cruz and Beto left in the van and Ivan in his pickup. Ernesto and Abel stood talking outside for a few minutes before leaving in their own vehicles.

"That was good, wasn't it?" Ernesto said.

"Yeah, man!" Abel said. "Paul has been there for us. Now finally we got the chance to come through for him. How about Ivan, though? I never figured him to do something like that."

172

"Ivan's a good guy," Ernesto asserted. "Paul told me Ivan told him he was really bullied all through school. He *is* kind of a nerd. But it didn't turn him bitter. He's a sweet guy. The bullying didn't turn him against people. It's like that quote my mom loves—she's always saying it. 'Life is ten percent what you make it, and ninety percent how you take it.'"

Ernesto wanted to ask Abel whether there was anything new in his life. Had he seen Claudia, maybe talked to her? But he didn't want to bring up the subject. He thought it was still too painful for Abel. But then, to Ernesto's surprise, Abel brought it up.

"I saw Claudia the other night," Abel confided.

"You did?" Ernesto couldn't think of anything else to say.

"Yeah. She said she'd broken up with Victor Toro," Abel responded. He stood with his hands in his pockets and head down. "I went to the doughnut shop at a slow time when I knew she'd have a chance to talk. I just wanted to know the score. I mean, we meant something to each other for a while. I needed to know . . ." Abel had a strange look on his face, not sad or angry, just a little numb.

"So what did you find out?" Ernesto asked.

"She didn't come right out and say it, but I think Toro wanted out," Abel replied. "I don't know what the deal was. I didn't ask. But she acted like he wanted the break."

"How do *you* feel, man?" Ernesto asked.

"Better," Abel said. "It was a heavy blow when she dumped me. It hurt a lot. The bruise got dark and swollen, but then the pain went down, little by little. I cared a lot for Claudia. I thought she cared for me. I was surprised at first that she liked me 'cause she's pretty. And she comes from a nice family. I kept thinking, 'Pinch yourself, dude. Is this really happening to you?' She was out of my league, Ernie."

"Wait a minute, man," Ernesto said. He was going to do what he did so many times. He'd build Abel up, tell him what a great guy he was. But this time Abel cut him off.

"Come on, Ernie. It only makes it worse. I know who I am. I'm a plain-looking dude with a shy personality."

Abel glanced up from the ground and grinned at his friend. "Yeah, I'm a great chef. I know that. I can make meals over at the Sting Ray better than Pedro. I know what customers are saying. That chick over there, she says I'm a genius. I think maybe I'm going places, man. You built a fire under me that day. You pushed me to follow my dream. If you didn't do that, none of this would be happening. I'll always be grateful to you, Ernie, for that. Thanks, man, from the bottom of my heart."

"*Por nada*," Ernesto replied. "It was all in your heart and soul."

"But the fact is," Abel went on, "I couldn't keep Claudia. She got tired of me. She wanted a guy who was hotter, more exciting. That's why she fell for Toro. When I went in the doughnut shop, she was nice and friendly. She said she was sad that we broke up, but she wasn't interested in seeing me again."

"Did she say that?" Ernesto asked.

"Nah," Abel said with a shake of his head. "But I could tell she was ready for somebody else. She didn't want the same old, same old. I don't either. I just wanted to talk to her and let her know I didn't have any hard feelings. I got my pride. I didn't want her to think I'd heard of her and Toro splitting. Now here I was like a dog with my tongue hanging out, panting for her again. I'm not saying it doesn't still hurt. It'll hurt for a long time. But I'm okay. Paul gave me the best advice in all this. He said to never let her see me bleed, and I didn't. I never did. I'm proud of that."

"Yeah," Ernesto agreed, "Paul got it right."

"Me and Bianca, we got a nice friendship going," Abel went on. He was half talking over his shoulder to Ernesto. "We don't want anything complicated. She likes a funny movie once in a while. I do too. She's right for me now. Neither of us have the hots for each other. That's good. You can't get burned if you don't have the hots, you know?" Abel smiled a little as he started to get into his Jetta.

"Dude!" Ernesto called out, pointing both index fingers at Abel. "You're the best friend I ever had, and don't you ever forget that."

Abel's smiled deepened. "Likewise, homie."

Before Abel started up the engine, he leaned out the window and slapped the driver's side door. Then he said to Ernesto, "Hey, your mom's lizard book was just published, man. How about if I come over a week from tomorrow —Sunday—and make a celebration meal for the occasion? I'd enjoy doing that. If Paul's brother is out by then, we'll invite them over too if your folks are okay with that."

"Man, one of your dinners is always something to look forward to, Abel," Ernesto agreed. "And it would be a good way to welcome David home. David's got to be feeling like a fish out of water when he gets out of that place. It would mean a lot to Paul too."

"A dinner of good old *carne asada* with *nopales*, black beans and grilled onions, zucchini, tomatoes, and plantains. What d'ya think? Just the thing to help the dude forget the sound of slamming steel doors." Abel ticked off the menu as he hung out the car window.

"Yeah," Ernesto agreed enthusiastically. "I'm hungry now, man. I've never been in the slammer, but I understand the food isn't too good."

"Lotsa bologna sandwiches from what I heard from a couple homies who did time," Abel laughed.

"Goodnight, Abel," Ernesto said. "I feel really great about what we did here."

"Night, homie," Abel said as the Jetta's engine began to purr. "Me too. It was one of our finest hours." He laughed again.

As Ernesto walked to his Volvo, he had a warm feeling that Abel Ruiz was on the mend. He had survived a broken heart, and he had come out stronger than ever.

CHAPTER TEN

As Ernesto drove home in the Volvo, he started to figure out how he would break the news to his parents. Abel was going to cook Sunday dinner, which they would love. And maybe Paul and his ex-con brother would be coming too, which might give them pause.

When Ernesto got home, his father was mowing the front lawn. Drought had hit southern California over the past several years. So Dad had shrunk the size of the lawn. Large parts of it were gravel, where gray-green cacti that needed little water thrived. It looked good, and Dad could cut the small patch of grass in no time.

"Hi, Ernie," Dad hailed. "You guys get Paul's apartment all fixed up for when his brother comes?"

"Yeah, and you know what happened?" Ernesto was eager to report. "You know Ivan Redondo, Lourdes Ibarra's husband? He brought a brand-new bed and a chest of drawers for David. We were all blown away. Paul would strangle me if he heard me saying this, but I think I saw tears in his eyes."

"What a beautiful gesture from Ivan," Luis Sandoval declared. "Emilio thinks the world of Ivan. He says he's the finest son-in-law a man could have."

That comment only made Ernesto more nervous about what he had to say. Dad and Emilio Ibarra got together often because they had been childhood friends. Every time they did, Mr. Ibarra no doubt shared his apprehensions about his beloved Carmen selecting Paul Morales instead of some nice, nerdy clone like Ivan Redondo.

"Abel wants to come over next Sunday and cook us some great *carne asada*," Ernesto announced cheerfully. "He'll tell us what to buy, and then he'll cook it to perfection like he always does. He said he wants to celebrate Mom's getting her new book published."

"Is that great, or what?" Dad exclaimed happily, his face beaming. "Abel is such a wonderful boy. Maria will be so touched."

"Dad . . . uh . . . do you think it'd be okay if we invited Paul and Carmen too?" Ernesto asked, believing it was best to ease into the whole question.

"Sure," Luis Sandoval agreed. "I understand how Emilio feels about Paul, but I like him. He's a straight-up guy."

Ernesto was feeling a little weakness in his legs. He tried to screw up his courage. "Oh . . . and Dad . . . Paul's brother might be getting out of prison this week, you know. Paul's planning to pick him up on Wednesday and . . ." Ernesto had a very dry throat and the words came out with difficulty. "Well maybe . . . you know . . ."

Luis Sandoval smiled. "You'd like for David to come to dinner too, right?"

"Yeah. It'd mean so much to Paul," Ernesto said. "I mean this guy—David—he's been in there for several years. He's got to feel weird right now. He's been doing really well there, not breaking any rules. He's getting a college education, going to all the programs they asked him to. He's getting out really early because all the people there said he's been rehabilitated. But still, to be coming back into the real world all of a sudden has got to be scary for the guy. I haven't even told Paul about the dinner yet. I wanted to see if you and Mom were okay with it first."

"*Mi hijo*," Dad spoke gently. "I have no objections, but I'm not sure how your mother would feel about it. You want me to ask her, or do you want to?"

Ernesto really wanted to push the job of asking Mom on Dad. But he knew in his

183

heart that that wasn't fair. Paul Morales was *his* friend. Even though Mom was initially turned off by him, she tolerated him for Ernesto's sake. She frowned every time she saw the rattlesnakes on his hand. Now that Ernesto wanted to bring Paul's ex-con brother to the Sandoval dinner table, it was Ernesto's job to tell her.

"Thanks for the offer, Dad, but I'll ask Mom," Ernesto replied.

Luis Sandoval looked relieved.

Ernesto thought a lot about how he would approach his mother. Under most circumstances, Ernesto had no problem at all talking to his mother about anything. However, he still felt closer to his father because he was easier to talk to in tricky situations. Maria Sandoval was a good-hearted, compassionate person, but she was very protective of her family. Ernesto feared Mom wouldn't be happy about having an ex-prisoner sitting at the dinner table with her family, especially her two little girls, and her elderly mother-in-law.

The more Ernesto thought about it, the more nervous he became. Maybe, he thought, the whole idea was bad. Even if Mom agreed, would she act so horrified that it would set David Morales back instead of helping? Maybe David looked awful, with that prison pallor some ex-cons have, the gray, haunted look of men who'd lived behind bars.

Maybe Katalina and Juanita would be scared.

Ernesto sat in the living room, sinking into the sofa and closing his eyes. He was trying to collect his thoughts. He was about ready to text Abel and tell him it wasn't going to work.

"Ernie!" Mom's voice snapped Ernesto alert. She sat down beside him on the sofa.

"Oh hi, Mom," Ernesto said.

Mom reached over and gently shoved a cowlick off Ernesto's brow. Her hands felt like silk. Even in the darkened living room, she looked beautiful. "Sweetheart, you look like you're carrying the weight of the world on your shoulders. Are you all right?" she asked.

"Uh, I kinda did something stupid," Ernesto replied.

"All right. Whatever it is, it isn't the end of the world. Tell me what stupid thing you did, Ernie," Mom asked, smiling a little.

In a strange way, Ernesto felt as though he was five years old again. He had been playing baseball with his friends in Los Angeles, and they'd just sent a ball crashing through Mom's picture window. Ernesto thought then he was in the worst trouble of his life, but Mom just laughed and forgave him.

"Abel had this weird idea, and I sort of went along with it," he confided. "Now I see I shouldn't have because it's crazy." Ernesto began thinking he was better off just getting it all out. "Abel wants to cook *carne asada* for us on Sunday to celebrate your new book getting published. But, see, he wants to invite Paul and Carmen too. So that's one thing, but there's something else.

He wants to invite Paul's brother, David. He's getting out of prison. But that'd be crazy, and I should have told Abel right away . . ."

Mom's eyes grew larger, but the smile did not completely leave her lips. "Is Paul's brother dangerous?" she asked.

"Oh no, Mom!" Ernesto answered. "He was convicted of burglarizing some stores at night, but he was never violent. He never hurt anybody. Not even close. He's been in prison for two years. He got a kind of junior college education in that time and did everything they asked him to do. He never missed Bible study. He got real religious. I mean, Ivan Redondo told me he was one of the best students he had 'cause, you know, Ivan teaches Bible at the prison. Carmen has visited him, and she said he's really nice and everything."

"He sounds way better than Paul," Mom remarked, laughing a little. "Maybe we should let him come and keep Paul away."

Ernesto could never remember a time in his life that he didn't love his mother. But there were special moments, like now, when he loved her so much. He could hardly contain his gratitude at having Maria Sandoval for a mom. Ernesto reached out and hugged his mother, and she giggled like a girl.

Mom asked, "What about your father? Have you asked him?"

Ernesto replied, "Yeah, I did. And he kinda said . . ."

Mother and son looked at each other for a split second. Then both said at the same time, "Ask your mother."

Ernesto rushed outside where his father was putting the lawn mower away in the small shed. "Dad, you sure knew how to pick 'em!" he cried.

Luis Sandoval laughed. "She okayed it, huh? I thought she would."

Ernesto texted Abel that dinner was on. Then he called Paul. "Paul, you got anything special going on Sunday?"

"Well, I get David on Wednesday," Paul responded. "We'll be busy getting him new clothes. I guess by Sunday I'll take the poor devil out to a nice restaurant to eat. He hasn't had a good feed in a while."

"How about dinner at the Sandovals? Abel's cooking, dude," Ernesto suggested.

There was a long silence at the other end of the line. Then Paul answered, "You serious, man?"

"Yeah, Paul," Ernesto said.

"Your folks . . . they . . ." Paul began.

"Dad said yes right away, but Mom thought about it for a minute. After I told her about David, she wanted him to come but she wasn't so sure about you," Ernesto said. He could hear nothing then but Paul laughing.

Ernesto called Carmen with the news.

"Oh, Ernie, that's so cool," she gasped.

"It was Abel's idea, but I went for it. Dad was okay with it right away. I thought I'd have to sell it to Mom, but she blew me away by saying yes quick," Ernesto said.

"You got nice parents, Ernie, and they got a pretty awesome *hijo*," Carmen told him.

The following afternoon, Ernesto took Katalina and Juanita for sundaes at the new yogurt shop on Washington. The girls thought that this was a grand gesture of generosity. But Ernesto had an ulterior motive. He had to make sure they understood who was coming to dinner on Sunday. He didn't want them to blurt out something embarrassing. Ernesto never cared what the girls said in front of Paul because he indulged them and laughed everything off. But David would be tense and nervous. Ernesto didn't want the girls to say something that would hurt him.

As they sat in a booth waiting for their sundaes, Ernesto said, "Abel is gonna make *carne asada* for us Sunday. He wants to celebrate Mom getting her lizard book published."

"Oh wow," Katalina exclaimed. "I love it when Abel cooks."

"Me too," Juanita chimed in.

"Paul and Carmen are coming too," Ernesto told them.

Katalina giggled. "I love it when Paul makes the rattlesnake on his hand jump. It's like it's alive! It makes me scream, but I love it."

"I like Paul," Juanita added. "He's funny."

The sundaes were delivered. They looked beautiful with snowy peaks of whipped cream and bright red cherries. Ernesto gave his sisters a few moments to dig into the sundaes. Then he said, "Paul's brother, David, is coming too."

"Did we ever meet David?" Katalina asked as she picked a cherry from her sundae.

"No, I've never met him either," Ernesto replied. "But Carmen has, and she said he's really nice. See, David has been away for two years."

"Why?" Juanita asked. "Was he in the army? I bet he's a soldier. You know what Mom does every time she sees a boy or girl in a uniform? She walks right up to them and says, 'Thank you for serving.' I like that. Daddy was a soldier, and he was so brave."

"Daddy has a war scar on his face," Katalina said. "Mama says we've got to thank all the soldiers and marines and sailors for making us safe."

"I bet Mama will thank David for serving too," Juanita said.

Ernesto felt really uncomfortable. He somehow did not introduce this subject well. He wished he could say that David Morales just got back from the war. That would make things easy. A war hero was coming to eat at the Sandoval table. The girls would connect with that.

"Kat, Juanita, I have to tell you something very serious and I want you to listen hard, okay?" Ernesto told them. "This is hard for me to explain, and you have to help me."

The girls looked intently at Ernesto, even pausing in eating their sundaes. They were used to their brother smiling most of the time. Now he looked almost grim. "You know that Paul was raised in foster homes, don't you?" Ernesto asked.

"Yeah," Katalina responded. "He told us his parents weren't there, so the county sent them around to different homes. I thought that was really awful."

"I'd hate for that to happen to me," Juanita said fretfully.

"Well, Paul and his older brother David were sent to foster homes when Paul was nine and David was twelve," Ernesto started to explain. "They were sent to a lot of foster homes because things didn't work out. The families didn't want the boys or something. David and Paul lived in different foster homes, and they didn't get to see each other much. The boys didn't get much love. But even though they were separated, they loved each other. Paul and David were the only family either one of them had."

The girls were totally into Ernesto's story, and he continued. "You know how you've got Mom and Dad and *Abuela*, and Mom's parents, and me and your uncles and aunts? You've got a lot of people to love you. You know how *Tía* Hortencia hugs you when she sees you? And how Uncle Arturo lifts you up in the air and tells you how beautiful you are? How Grandma and Grandpa Vasquez bring you gifts when they come? Well, Paul and David didn't have any of that. They had a hard time as kids."

Both Katalina's and Juanita's eyes were large and sad now. They were both compassionate kids. Their teachers told their parents that the girls would always reach out to a child whom the other children were ignoring. They felt sorry for the underdog, whether it was another child or a stray animal. Ernesto thought his parents were doing a good job raising them.

"Paul is strong and tough," Ernesto told the girls. "So even though he had a bad childhood, he was able to make a good life. David got messed up. He got in trouble with the law because he was mixed up with bad friends. He stole stuff from stores and got arrested."

Katalina looked guilty. "One time I stole a candy bar from the twenty-four-seven store," she confessed. "And Mr. Hussam caught me. I was so scared. Mama made me apologize and stuff. I never stole anything again."

"Well, David stole big stuff," Ernesto explained. "Then he sold it and made money. He sneaked into stores at night and stole stuff, and he got in big trouble. He was about twenty-one, and they sentenced him to five years in prison."

"Paul's brother was in prison for five years?" Katalina asked, wide-eyed.

"No, he's been in prison for two years. He worked hard to prove that he was sorry and he meant to do better. He took classes and got a college degree. He worked in the prison cafeteria and did everything they told him to do. He went to Bible study classes to learn to be a better man. All the people at the prison said he had improved himself more than anybody they ever saw. So they let him out earlier, but he'll be on parole for a while. That means he has to visit with his parole officer and prove that he's leading an good life."

"What if he makes another mistake?" Katalina asked.

"Then he'll be sent back to prison to serve his full five years and maybe more," Ernesto answered. "But David is determined to never break the law again. He's really sorry for what he did. The prison people said he's rehabilitated. That means he's like a new man starting over a fresh life."

"Is David in prison right now?" Juanita asked.

"Yes," Ernesto replied. "On Wednesday, Paul is going to the prison to pick him up and bring him home. Me and Abel and Cruz and Beto all worked with Paul on Saturday to fix up the apartment. So there's a place for David to stay. Ivan Redondo—do you remember him? He's Carmen's brother-in-law, he's married to Carmen's sister, Lourdes—"

Juanita giggled. "He's funny. He likes opera. He played some opera for me. Everybody was screaming."

"Well, Ivan came over to help make David's room too. He even brought a nice new bed and a chest of drawers for David," Ernesto said.

"That was nice," Katalina commented.

"Girls, Paul is so happy to have his brother home with him," Ernesto told them. "He missed his brother so much. He visited him as often as he could in prison. When I told Paul that he and David were invited to come to our house on Sunday, he couldn't believe it. He was so excited. Are you girls going to be okay with David coming?"

"Ah yes, Ernie," Katalina responded. "If he's Paul's brother, I'll be extra nice to him. I feel bad that him and Paul didn't have a happy time when they were kids. We'll try to make it up by being nice to David."

"Yeah," Juanita added. "We won't say anything that would make David feel bad."

"You're great," Ernesto said. "I knew uld count on you. But I wanted you now everything so you wouldn't be rised."

ıtalina got a very serious look on her face then. "You know what, Ernie? Last month we got a new student in my class," she began. "The teacher told us all about him before he came. She said him and his parents were camping, and the trailer burned. Our teacher told us his face was scarred, and she told us not to treat him funny because of that."

Juanita asked, "So what happened?"

"Everybody was good when Austin came to school," Katalina answered. "He was really scared that the kids would make fun of him or something. But we treated him just like anyone else. Now most of us don't even see the scars 'cause Austin is a lot of fun. He plays baseball real good. I guess Paul's brother is scarred on the inside because of what happened to him. But it's gonna be okay 'cause if he's Paul's brother we wanna make him happy in our house."

Ernesto smiled at Katalina. Just now she seemed much older than her years. Right now he was bursting with pride.

Then Juanita asked, "Does he have any tattoos like Paul and Cruz?"

"I'm not sure," Ernesto replied, "but I don't think so."

"I like tattoos," Juanita remarked. "Maybe David could get a rattlesnake like Paul has, and they could both jump." Juanita giggled.

The girls began talking about what Abel was going to cook. They loved his meals.

Ernesto looked at his little sisters. He breathed a huge sigh of relief. He wondered why he ever worried at all about how they'd treat David Morales.

Ernesto spooned some ice cream and topping into his mouth. He felt as though he had learned a lesson. He always thought he was pretty good at reading people. He'd had dark suspicions about Roxanne, and he was right about her. She *was* lying to the police. He'd had no such suspicions about

Griff, and he was right again. Griff *wasn't* the shooter.

But Ernesto wasn't right all the time. He'd suspected Claudia Villa of being a heartless gold digger. But she wasn't such a bad person. She was just shallow and self-centered. In the end, she was badly hurt by Victor Toro. And Ernesto should have had more dark suspicions about Cabron, and he didn't. That mistake could have cost him his life.

Now, he realized, he'd had unfair suspicions about David Morales. And Ernesto's two little sisters had just shown him how wrong he probably was about David too.

"I guess," Ernesto thought, "You have to be careful about suspecting people of bad things. Sometimes you're right. But when you're wrong, you're just being plain unfair to them."

Ernesto took another spoonful of sundae. "OK," he thought to himself, "lesson learned."